# katie's two
wars

a novel by
Barbara Azore

For Jacqueline Spencer

Barbara Azore
February 2015

 **FriesenPress**

Suite 300 - 990 Fort St
Victoria, BC, Canada, V8V 3K2
www.friesenpress.com

Copyright © 2015 by Barbara Azore
First Edition — 2015

2-5855-2 (Hardcover)
2-5856-9 (Paperback)
5857-6 (eBook)

Var & Military

he trade by The Ingram Book Company

DEDICATION

This Book Is Dedicated to my Father,
Who was a teenage machine gunner in the trenches of the
First World War and a sailor on a Naval minesweeper in the second.
and to
Andrew James Chamberlain
My amazing, beloved son, a loving husband,
father and brother. He was taken from us too
soon and will be missed by all who knew him.

ACKNOWLEDGEMENTS

Thanks to:

Tim Bowling, novelist and poet, Writer-In-Residence at the University of Aberta;

Mary Dawe (1926 - 2014), writer and teacher of writing;

Linda Goyette, journalist, writer of children's stories, a Writer-In-Residence at Edmonton Public Library and

Brelan Boyce who helped a not very knowledgeable computer person to get published,

for their advice and encouragement.

TABLE OF CONTENTS

PROLOGUE

May 8th, 2005. I am watching television in my Canadian apartment. It is showing Queen Elizabeth attending a ceremony to celebrate the ending of the Second World War in Europe.

On that day in 1945 I did not know what the future would bring, but when it came I was sure that there would be another war in it.

It is sixty years since the war ended, and I was a child living in the outskirts of London.

Back then, I could not remember a time when there was not a war being fought and I knew from my history books that the First World War had ended only twenty-seven years before the second one started. I told my sister Helen my twelve-year-old's fear that another atomic bomb would set the war machine in motion once again. She, twelve years older than I, assured me that there would not be another war. Time thus far has proved us both wrong. We have come close to what I feared. The Cuban crisis took us to the brink and the threat of the means to make the bomb being in the hands of unscrupulous leaders hangs like Damocles' sword over us still. There has not been another World War but fighting between groups and countries constantly erupts like volcanoes around the globe.

I am an old lady now and while I sometimes cannot recall what I did this morning, I remember the 1939-1945 War as though it was yesterday. Our peaceful, pre-war life suddenly erupted with new laws and regulations, homes were destroyed, and families were uprooted and divided. While I am still waiting for World Peace to break out, I would like to tell you how the war affected me in more ways than one.

PART ONE

Chapter 1

BEFORE THE WAR

My first six years of life were happy ones, living with my parents, my eighteen-year-old sister, Helen, and a small menagerie of animals, in Hounslow, which in 1939 was in the County of Middlesex, England. Middlesex has since been swallowed up by London so now Hounslow is in a borough of the London County Council.

I shared a garden pond with goldfish year-round and in the spring and summer; frogs; a small tortoise who slowly plodded around the lawn and flowerbeds and in a corner of the garden; two cages of guinea pigs who multiplied so fast that my mother took the babies to the pet shop every few weeks and exchanged them for goldfish. Lucy, a cat, and Ollie, a dog, shared the house and garden with me.

While Lucy liked to sit watching and sometimes trying to catch the fish, Ollie was intrigued by Trot, my tortoise. When Ollie approached, Trot disappeared into her shell. Ollie would walk round and round her, trying to poke his nose or a paw into her shell. When that failed, he would flip her onto her back When she still remained hidden, he would finally give up until the next time he came across her slowly walking in the garden.

Ollie was a small, brown dog with a thin tail that pointed to the sky. He was of unknown pedigree or as my mother called him, a Heinz-57. He was my father's dog and accepted my mother because she was the one who fed him, but when I was born Ollie was very old and was jealous of the attention I received. He knew that if he bit me he would be in trouble with my mother. That did not stop him snarling at me if I got too close.

I was not the only person he disliked. He was never taken for a walk in the street because he had a nasty habit of snapping at the ankles of anyone who passed him. The coalman was his particular enemy. Perhaps it was because the coal dust in the sacks of coal the coalman carried turned him black from head to feet. When he came to deliver our coal, Mother shut Ollie in the front hallway. I remember one day when things went badly wrong.

I was upstairs when the coalman knocked at the back door for his money. I had not noticed him arrive, so I ran down the stairs to see who was visiting. Ollie was standing at the door into the kitchen. As soon as I opened it he streaked past me and dived between my mother's legs. I ran after him and arrived at the back door to see the coalman on the outside of the front gate and on the inside, Ollie, hanging on to the man's trouser leg, pulling with all his might. Mother clamped her hands over my ears so that I would not hear what the coalman was shouting at Ollie. He had taken off his headgear, a cap with a long piece of cloth hanging down to protect his back when he was carrying the sacks of coal, and he was slapping Ollie with it. They both disappeared in the clouds of coal dust that rose around them. Mother stopped covering my ears and ran to pull Ollie off the man's leg. There was a loud sound of tearing cloth as the bottom of the coalman's trouser leg was ripped away. Still muttering loudly, he made his escape and climbed onto the coal wagon. He slapped the reins of his two huge Clydesdale horses and made a hasty retreat.

Mother soundly scolded Ollie but he trotted off covered in coal dust, with tail held high and the cloth from the coalman's trousers held proudly in his jaws. Mother looked almost as black as the coalman and brushing her hair out of her eyes only made matters worse. I wanted to laugh but my mother looked so mad I did not dare to do so. When my father came home that evening and Mother told him what had happened, he did laugh until she told him that Ollie was banned from the house until he had been bathed. "And you," she said poking her finger at his chest, "are going to do the bathing." Being bathed was another thing Ollie hated.

I helped Father get the old metal tub from the shed and he filled it with warm water from the kitchen. The first thing we had to do was find Ollie. He was not in his dog kennel. We looked under the bushes and behind the coal shed and the wash house. He seemed to have disappeared. It was getting darker by the minute. "This is like looking for a black cat on a moonless night," Father grumbled.

That gave me an idea. Lucy, the cat, was my mother's pet. Lucy no doubt felt the same way about Ollie as Ollie did about me. Fully grown, he was not much bigger than the cat and had learned early that getting too close to Lucy got his nose clawed. It was funny to watch them together. When Lucy was sleeping in her favourite chair, Ollie would put his nose against her, prod her, and leap back out of reach. If she was lying in his path, he walked crabwise around her at a safe distance. When there was not room to get around her, he waited patiently until she moved. I often watched Lucy wait in hiding for Ollie to come along, and then leap out at him. Poor Ollie would jump in the air and run away as fast as his short legs could carry him.

I said, "Perhaps Lucy could find him."

At that moment, Ollie suddenly burst onto the path with Lucy in pursuit. He saw Father and me, swerved to avoid us, and slipped headlong into the pond. Lucy skidded to a halt and ignoring us, walked sedately into the house as though the commotion was nothing to do with her.

Laughing, Father grabbed Ollie's collar and pulled him out of the water. "Ollie old boy, it looks as though you have bathed yourself. Come on, we'll just rinse the pond water off in the tub and dry you. You'd better hope the fish don't swallow the coal dust or we'll both be in the doghouse."

Life was full of surprises and fun before the war began.

I started school in September 1938, when I was five years old. Mother went with me the first day and we were joined by our neighbours Jimmy and Dougie King and their mother. Jimmy was starting school too. Dougie was only four and would start school next year. Our mothers had to register us with the school secretary. When my turn came, my mother mentioned that I could already read.

The secretary looked at her as though she had said that I had two heads. "You shouldn't teach a child to read," she admonished. "You don't do it correctly." The other waiting mothers tut-tutted and looked disapprovingly at Mother and me.

I felt sorry for Mother and tried to defend her. "Mummy didn't teach me," I protested, "my sister did." Actually no one had taught me. Helen used to read to me and I looked at, and remembered, the words as she read them. Somehow I knew that the secretary would never believe that. She looked even more annoyed. Deprived of anyone to blame she stated, "Kate will be in Room One. Show her where that is and then go."

Mother took me to the door of Room One, where Jimmy and his mother were saying goodbye. Mother kissed me, and Jimmy and I waved to our mothers as they left. We looked at one another and warily ventured into the classroom, stopping just inside the door. At the front of the room, a woman was sitting at a desk on a raised platform. She turned her head as we stood hesitating in the doorway.

"Don't stand there gawking," she said. "Sit in the first two desks in the third row."

Jimmy looked at me and made a face. We sat at our desks and Jimmy leaned toward me. "She's no fun," he whispered.

The teacher glared in our direction. "No talking in class," she barked.

The school was very old. My father and mother had gone there when they were children. The windows in the classroom were very high up the wall so that all one could see of the outside world was the sky. Bored, we sat in silence and waited while other children, some alone and others in groups, came into the classroom. When there was a child at every desk, the teacher closed the door and marched to the blackboard behind her. She wrote something on the board, rubbed her hands together to rub off the chalk, and turned to face us. "Good morning children," she said. "I am your teacher. Open your desks and take out the notebook and pencil you will find there."

The lids of some of the desks dropped with a crash.

"Quietly please," shouted the teacher. "Those of you whose lids are still up, put them down GENTLY."

I put mine down very gently, and placed the notebook and pencil on the top. There was a little groove in the top of the desks to hold pencils and pens and there were holes holding inkwells. The lids sloped gently downwards and of course some of the pencils rolled onto the floor. A scraping of chairs followed as children got up to retrieve the pencils.

The teacher rapped her desktop with a wooden cane. "That's enough of that. Sit down, face front, and be quiet." She pointed to the words on the board with the cane. "This is my name, Mrs Deane, and this is the room number. Can any of you read the room number?"

Murmurs of, "I can," or "I think so," ran around the room.

Mrs Deane thumped the desk again. "Don't shout out. Put up your hands."

I put up my hand. A few children put up both hands.

"One hand is quite sufficient thank you," said Mrs Deane.

I caught Jimmy's eye and we both grimaced. Mrs Deane definitely was not going to be much fun.

Chapter 2

1939 THE WAR BEGINS

A year after I started school, I remember sitting in the living room with Mother, Father, and Helen listening to a man on the radio announce that Britain had declared war on Germany. I did not know exactly what that meant, but I knew it was not a good thing. For weeks, the adults had been talking and worrying about a possible war and now that it had come, they seemed pleased. When the broadcast ended a siren began to wail, and our neighbours ran into the street, shouting and hugging one another. My parents and Helen joined them and I watched through the window, puzzled. If war was bad, why were they so happy? Looking back, I think the rejoicing was actually relief that the weeks of tension, watching Hitler's juggernaut swallowing Europe, apparently unopposed, had come to an end.

That was the third of September, 1939. On the first of September, the government had initiated an idea to send children from central London to the country, to keep them safe from the bombing. When the new school year began, the idea was put into practice. Many children were put onto trains and sent to the countryside. Here they were billeted with families who took them into their homes. Some of the children were very unhappy, and when the expected German bombers failed to materialise, large numbers of parents brought their children home again.

The second week of September the summer holidays ended and school started. Jimmy and I returned to school. We had told Dougie, who was going into year one, how horrible Mrs Deane was, and he made a terrible fuss when his mother had to drag him to the school the first day.

He was fine the next day because when Jimmy and I arrived at our new room, we found Mrs Deane sitting at the teacher's desk. A new young teacher was teaching the year one children.

The next morning when I set out for school, Jimmy called, "Wait for us Katie."

I stopped. "Hello, Jimmy, Dougie."

Jimmy and Dougie King lived with their mother, father and grandmother. Mr King walked with a limp. This, Dougie had explained to me, was why he had not been called up to fight in the war. Instead, he was an air raid warden – one of the men and women who made sure no lights were showing after dark.

"It's a very important job," Dougie told me proudly. "When a house is bombed he has to call for the fire engine and ambulance and try to help the people who were in the house when the bomb fell on it."

We made our way to school, balancing along the now-low garden walls that had once been topped by ornamental railings. The railings had been taken to factories to be made into planes and ships and tanks. We pinched our noses as we passed the smelly bin at the top of the road where the peelings and table scraps were collected for the farmers' pigs. Someone had painted, "Waste Not – Want Not" in red paint around the outside of the bin.

Now we could hear the children playing in the schoolyard. Then a bell started ringing. "Come on," Jimmy shouted. "We'll be late!"

My father had brought a map of the world home and put it up on the living room wall. He read the reports of what was happening in Europe in the morning papers, and listened to the radio news every night. He put coloured pins on the map to represent the different countries' armies; black for the enemy, red, blue, green, and white for our allies. Every day it seemed the number of black pins increased and another colour disappeared.

The government gave everyone gas masks. They came in small cardboard boxes with long string handles to be worn over the shoulder. We were supposed to keep them with us at all times. Leaflets came to the house showing us how to put strips of brown sticky tape onto our windows. Father explained it was to stop the glass flying about if the window glass broke. At the time, I did not understand why our windows might get broken. The leaflets also told us that we had to cover our windows at night so that no light could be seen from the street. Father made boards to fit in the window frames and every evening, as soon as it began to get dark, they were put up before we turned on a light. "That's so the enemy planes won't see lights from the houses and know they are over a town," Father explained.

No planes did come immediately. I am sure the adults hoped they never would.

Chapter 3

1940 BLITZKRIEG

The year started badly. In January, everyone was given a ration book. This was a small paper book filled with coupons for food. Father had dug up the flowerbeds in the garden the previous fall, to enlarge his vegetable garden. Daffodils, tulips, pansies, marigolds, gladioli, and lupins were replaced with potatoes, carrots, peas, beans, cabbages, and sprouts. We were not going to starve.

Bacon, butter, and sugar were rationed on the eighth of January; on the eleventh of March, all meat, except sausages, was rationed, followed in July by tea and margarine. We had to register with the shops we would buy from. At a store, we had to hand over our ration books to the store keeper who either cut out a coupon or crossed it out to show that we had been given the week's allowance of whatever we had bought.

Tea was the most missed by the adults, at two ounces per person, per week, but I enjoyed buying our small ration of sugar the most. We were allowed eight ounces of sugar a person per week. Mother used one of our coupons each week and bought the sugar from an old lady who ran a small grocery store. The sugar was delivered to the shop in large sacks, which stood on the floor. A brass scale was on a small table beside one of the sacks and the shop lady sat on a stool between the two. She carefully weighed our eight ounces of sugar onto the scale, and carefully poured it into a paper bag, making sure that none spilled on the floor. The top of the paper bag was firmly folded over and placed in Mother's shopping basket. How precious that bag of sugar seemed.

As the days passed into spring, Lucy began behaving oddly. A bird could pluck a worm from the lawn inches from her nose and she would ignore it. She slept all the time. She refused to eat. Ollie was confused at this new Lucy and did not know how to behave around her. I went with Mother to the vet who said Lucy was just old.

"She'll probably die quietly in her sleep," he told my mother. "With this war, that might be a blessing. The animals don't understand what is happening."

"I don't think I do," said Mother.

We carried Lucy home and put her close to the fire. Ollie came to investigate. He poked her with his nose, and when she ignored him he whined. "He doesn't understand either," I said.

On the war front things were no better. In June, disaster struck when the Germans trapped the British and Allied Forces on the beaches of Dunkirk. If the men could not be rescued, our army would be sadly depleted and the way would be open for a German invasion of Britain. There was no way the English Navy alone could evacuate the men from Dunkirk in time to save them. Father was glued to the radio every minute that he was home, worrying that our fate was sealed, and the Germans would occupy his beloved homeland.

Then a miracle happened. The government called upon every civilian who owned a boat to cross the Channel and bring our soldiers back. The boat owners answered the call. Between May twenty-fourth and June fourth, braving shells from France, mines in the Channel, and death from the skies, an Armada of eight hundred and fifty boats comprised of life boats, fishing boats, yachts, and small sail boats, snatched more than 330,500 British and French troops from the beaches and carried them to England. The sigh of relief from the British Isles was probably palpable enough to have been felt in France. Hitler would have to take another tack to conquer Britain.

In July, Hitler decided to invade Britain and to do so, he wanted to secure the Channel before invading. From the tenth to the thirty-first of that month, squadrons of German fighter planes and bombers attacked convoys in the English Channel and ports along the coast. The planes of the Royal Air Force were outnumbered, but suffered fewer losses than the German planes. Radar enabled the airports to know in advance of the German planes' approach. Every day, the same battles were fought with the same results. On the thirty-first of July, the Battle of Britain ended. In a speech to Parliament, Churchill, referring to the young men who had fought and lost their lives, spoke the words that went around the world: "Never in the field of human conflict was so much owed by so many to so few." The invasion was launched on August thirteenth, when seventy-four German bombers and fifty fighting planes crossed the channel, intending to bomb the southern coast of England. This was repeated every day. On September seventh, German planes began dropping bombs on London. The fires created in the East End of London burned into the next day and the Cockneys were the first to experience what became known as the Blitz.

There were anti-aircraft guns on the local heath and when the planes came over, we heard them firing. A wailing siren warned that enemy aircraft were coming. Father, Mother, Helen, and I huddled together in the small cupboard under the stairs until the ALL CLEAR sounded. There was headroom for only one adult at the entrance to the cupboard so that Father, Mother, or Helen had to stoop or crouch down on the floor. I had a small children's wooden chair to sit on. Father said the cupboard under the stairs was the safest place to be because our house and the house next door each had its own outside wall, but had been built touching one another. Often the only part left of a house that had been bombed was the staircase; a veritable ladder to heaven.

One day, some men came to our house and left sheets of corrugated iron and wooden bunks in the back garden. When father came home from work, he explained that this was going to be our shelter from bombs. I had seen bombs falling in the newsreels at the cinema. I could not imagine them falling on our house.

Father had to dig a big hole in the garden for the shelter. The instructions advised that the shelter should be put close to the house but father put ours at the bottom of the garden. "If the house gets hit it won't fall on the shelter," he said. I found my seaside spade and helped dig the hole. I was happily digging and throwing the dirt into the air when I heard father say, "Ouch!" I looked round. He was rubbing dirt from the back of his neck and inside his shirt.

"I'm sorry Katie but I'm afraid you are a bit too short for this work. You're supposed to throw the dirt out of the hole not down my neck." He lifted me out of the hole and said, "Just watch, okay?"

When the hole was deep enough, father lined it with the sheets of corrugated iron and placed a rounded sheet on top for a roof. One of the end-pieces had an opening for us to get in and out, and he added a little addition to the doorway so that Ollie would have a place to sleep. To make the shelter stronger, he covered the whole thing with cement. Inside the shelter were four bunk beds; two on each side, one above the other. "Mummy and I will sleep on one side and you and Helen on the other," said Father. "I think you had better sleep on the lower bunk, Katie." I lay on its hard boards to test it. I could not wait to sleep in it.

Now that we had a bomb shelter, we went into it as soon as darkness fell. We could still hear the guns on the heath and the planes, but I felt safe in our little tin and concrete house. One evening, we had an adventure before we even reached the shelter.

Father was leading the way with his flashlight and the bedding. Mother followed him with the cocoa and cups, next I came along; my arms clutching books and crayons. Behind me, Helen was carrying Lucy and leading Ollie on his lead.

It was very dark, no moon or stars to lead us, and as yet, no noise from gunfire or thumping planes. Suddenly there was a shriek behind me that scared me half to death. Desperate splashing noises followed. Father, Mother, and I turned to see what had happened and father directed his flashlight in the direction of the shriek. Helen was sitting in the pond, water dripping down her face, and weed in her hair. Ollie was standing beside the pond, his lead trailing in the water.

Father pulled Helen out of the water and Mother said, "Quick, get back to the house or she will get pneumonia."

"Come on Ollie," I said. "We're going back indoors."

In the house, Mother scurried around getting towels and making Helen take off her wet clothes. No one was worrying about bombs anymore. It wasn't until Helen had dry clothes on that Mother suddenly said, "Where's Lucy?" We looked around for her. She didn't reply to calling, and searching for her proved only that she was not in the house. Father opened the kitchen door to go to look for her and nearly fell over her. She had been sitting on the step, waiting for someone to open the door. Mother bent to stroke her. "Poor Lucy," she began, feeling sorry for her. She suddenly stopped. "Why she isn't even damp. She must have jumped over the pond." Laughing, she said, "Why didn't you think of that Helen?"

It took us a few minutes to get over the excitement and then we set out again on the trek to the shelter.

"Mind the pond," Father called out as he passed it. He was not going to let Helen forget that night for a long time.

Because Father had cemented over our shelter, I thought it looked like an igloo. I loved to play in it pretending to be an Eskimo, as the Inuit were called when I was a child. I had learned about these Arctic people in school. When a house was bombed, pieces of broken slate were left in the rubble. These made perfect spears and arrowheads when bound onto the end of a stick. On summer days, I dressed up in Mother's old fur coat and, armed with my spear, hunted for seals in the pond. I took my imaginary catch to the shelter and sat in the cool 'igloo,' nibbling on the stub of a candle or as I thought of it, 'blubber.'

The King family had a shelter, not an underground Anderson shelter like ours, but a rectangular brick building, which was above ground. It was a Morrison shelter, a smaller version of the ones on street corners for people who didn't have a garden, and pedestrians caught out in the street during a raid. The Kings never slept in it. I thought it was a dull thing and not a good place to play in. I wondered if that was why the Kings did not use it, but Jimmy said it was because his grandmother refused to sleep anywhere but in her own bed in her own bedroom. No silly little man in Europe was going to turn her out of her bed. He and Dougie slept with their mother and father under the dining room table.

When the bombing continued, Father became more and more despondent. I knew that as a young man he had fought in the 1914-18 war, so he was old enough to not be called up for active service. He became very quiet and spent all his spare time staring at the map of Europe with its pins marking how the battles were going, and listening to the news on the radio. We went to the movie house every week where the newsreel showed soldiers marching, and tanks rolling in one direction along the country roads of Europe, and people carrying their household goods in carts and on their backs, moving in the opposite direction. Sometimes we saw ships sinking in the sea and houses being bombed.

In my bunk at night, I could hear Mother and Father whispering to one another. I could not hear what was being said, but it did not sound good. Father became more and more upset. One evening as we were eating our meal he said, "I served a woman in the bank today whose son is in the Navy. She said he is stationed at Portsmouth and comes home every weekend."

Mother made no comment and kept on eating. Father spoke again.

"If I could get into the Navy, I might be sent to Portsmouth." Mother glared at him. I looked from one to the other. Mother's face was white, father's red. "Beth." He was pleading now. "I have nothing against the German people. Their soldiers in the last war fought bravely and well. They will be hard to beat. I saw what happened to France in the First World War. You don't want to have German soldiers marching along the roads of Britain. Hitler is a madman and must be stopped. I want to help to do that if I can."

Mother sighed. She looked near to tears. She put down her knife and fork and with a sigh stood up. "All right, you win. If you must go, go. The children and I will manage on our own." She turned to me and held out her hand. "Come along Katie. It's time to get ready to go to the shelter."

I looked at Father. He did not look as though he had won. He looked as though he had lost.

I took a long time to get undressed and into my pyjamas. I heard Mother going into the bathroom and then to the bedroom. Father was banging pots and pans together in the kitchen. Later, he slowly climbed the stairs and I heard him and mother talking. They were not shouting so I decided all was well again. We walked to the shelter in silence and mother made me get into my bunk straight away. I closed my eyes but could not sleep. Mother and Helen started knitting and Father read the newspaper. The only sound was the clicking of the needles and the rustle of the paper. Nobody spoke. I sensed the tension hanging like a pall over my head. When the siren went, Helen and Mother put their knitting away and climbed into their bunks. Father continued to read until the guns on the heath boomed into action. I pulled my blankets over my head and eventually fell asleep.

Father had left for work when I got up the next morning. Mother was quiet and looked tired and unhappy. When I came home from school at lunchtime, I was surprised to see father sitting at the dining table. He called to me. "Come here Katie. I have something to tell you." He patted his knee and lifted me onto his lap. "I'm sorry about what happened last night. Mummy and I have talked and agreed that I should do my bit to end this war. You and Helen and Mummy won't be safe until it is over. So, I have been to the recruiting office and I am going to be a sailor. I hope I will be able to come home to see you, but if I can't, I will write to you. Do you understand?"

I nodded. "I think so but I will miss you," I mumbled, trying not to cry.

"And I will miss you and Mummy, but we have to win this war. If that means me being away for a while, then it will be worth it."

15

A terrible thought crossed my mind.

"Mummy won't have to go to win the war will she?"

Father clutched me to him laughing. "No Katie. Mummy's going to win the peace."

Father decided that we should get rid of the guinea pigs. "They'll be too much for you to look after," he told Mother. He put them in a cardboard box and I went with him to the pet store. The owner was not too happy to be given so many guinea pigs. "People aren't buying pets these days," he grumbled. "They are having them put down because they can't feed 'em."

"I don't want anything for them," said father. "I'm going into the navy and I don't want to leave these for the wife to care for. She'll have enough problems without them." Still grumbling, the man took the box and, sadly, father and I went home.

It was a sad, grey day when my Mother and I went to the railway station to see father off to Portsmouth. Helen had said her goodbyes before she went to work.

The train came snorting along the platform, and pulled to a stop in a cloud of steam. Father bent down and gave me a big hug. "Bye-bye Katie. Be good for Mummy."

I clung to him crying. He gently loosened my hands from his neck and took Mummy into his arms. They kissed and when the train whistle blew, parted slowly, holding hands until father was on the train and the guard closed the carriage door. Father rolled down the window and put his head and arm out. The guard blew his whistle again, steam spurted from the train engine, and the wheels began to turn. Slowly at first, then gathering speed, the train began to chug away from us. Father waved from the train window. Mother ran beside it until the platform ended and then stood there waving, until the train disappeared around a bend. Slowly she walked back to where I was standing.

"Well it's just us and Helen now, Katie. We'll look after each other until this war is over and Daddy comes home again. Everything will be fine, I know it will."

A few days later, a letter arrived from father. He was going to come home on the weekend, before being posted. He wasn't allowed to tell us where he was to be sent but actually, he went as far away from London as was possible without leaving British waters.

His first posting was on a ship in Scapa Flow, Scotland.

The next morning, I found Mother sitting on the floor in the kitchen. She had Lucy on her lap. She was crying. I ran to her and looked at Lucy; she was quite still and her eyes were closed.

"What's wrong with Lucy, Mummy?"

"Oh, Katie. Lucy has died like the vet said she might."

I stroked Lucy's head. She looked as though she was sleeping. I had never seen anything dead before. I remembered how she used to curl up on my bunk at night and purr. It had made me feel safe. A tear fell as I realised she would never do that again. Mother got up. "We'll have to bury her, Katie. Will you help me?"

I fetched father's spade from the shed, and Mother dug a hole under the rose bush. She had wrapped Lucy in the blanket from her basket. She carefully placed her in the hole saying, "Goodbye, little friend."

Mother took my hand and we went back to a house that felt a little emptier because Lucy was not in it. When Helen came home from work she cried too, for Lucy and Mother.

Father arrived on the following Saturday, and Mother told him the sad news about Lucy. We showed him where we had buried her and he picked a rose and added it to the ones we had placed on the grave. He said he would like to stay in the garden a while. Helen took my hand and said, "We'll go inside and lay the table for lunch, Katie." Mother stayed behind with father and we left them holding hands.

Father had come home with a suitcase, in addition to his kitbag. When he and Mother came in, I asked him what was in it.

"Ah well, let me show you." He picked up the suitcase and opened it. Inside were a lot of winkles.

"I collected these this morning after breakfast. I thought you would like to have some for tea like we used to before the war. I was so busy wading around on the beach to pluck them off the rocks that I lost track of the time. When I checked my watch, I realised that I would have to hurry if I was to get to Portsmouth Station in time to catch the train to London."

"I left immediately but when I reached the station, the train was already getting ready to leave. I ran down the platform, which jiggled the case so hard that the closures on the suitcase opened. The lid fell down, spewing a trail of winkles along the platform. I picked up as many as I could and shoved them back into the suitcase. I had to hold the lid closed and tuck the suitcase under my arm. A fellow sailor on the train saw what had happened and helpfully held open a carriage door for me to leap into the train."

That afternoon, Father cooked the winkles in a large pot of boiling water and we ate them for tea. What a treat, for neither the winkle man nor the ice-cream man came around the streets once the war started.

We often had winkles for Sunday tea before the war. Winkles, or periwinkles, were like land snails but they lived in the sea. Every Sunday afternoon, the winkle man would push his cart of winkles, shrimps and prawns around the streets, ringing a bell to let people know he was ready to sell. When we heard the bell, Mother would give me a bowl and some money to buy the winkles. They were measured in half or one-pint metal cups. I would buy one large cup of winkles or sometimes shrimps for the four of us.

Eating winkles was an art form. Mother gave each of us a washed dressmaker's pin to remove the winkle from its shell. There was a little brown 'door' over the entrance to the shell, which had to be removed by levering the pin under it. Then the pin was inserted into the snail's body, twisted to bring the snail around the bend of the shell, and pulled out. The snails were then placed on a slice of buttered bread, sprinkled with a little salt and pepper and if desired, a little vinegar. A second slice of buttered bread was placed on top. It all seems a bit horrendous to me now, but as a child it was a delicious sandwich.

On Sunday night we walked father back to the station. It was just as hard to say goodbye as it had been the first time and we waved to the train until it disappeared. "I suppose we will get used to this in time," said Mother sighing. "But I hope I don't have to."

The next weekend, I stood at the back door holding a dish of vegetables swimming in gravy.

"Ollie," I called.

Helen came up behind me. "You'll have to call louder than that," she said and shouted, "Olleee."

Ollie was losing his sight and hearing, but he heard Helen. He came trotting around the corner of the house. When he reached the dustbin, he stopped and sat down, head cocked on one side, pointed ears and sharp nose twitching eagerly. His thin tail thumped on the cement path.

Helen sighed. "Poor old thing. Come a bit further Ollie. We're here."

Ollie turned toward the sound of Helen's voice and obediently walked toward it. I squatted down and placed the dish in front of his feet.

Mother called from the kitchen, "Bring the dish in when he's finished, Katie."

Helen turned into the house. "I'll go and dry the dishes for Mum," she said.

Ollie lapped up the unappetizing food hungrily. "Poor old Ollie," I murmured. "You would really like some meat wouldn't you?" With Father gone, our meat ration was smaller. Now we had only rations for three people, which left little to feed to a dog. I remembered what the vet had said about people's pets.

Since Lucy died, Ollie seemed to have grown older. Mother said that for a dog he was an old man. I think he missed Lucy as much as Mother and I did. A truce had grown up between him and me. He did not snarl at me anymore. Now he was noisily scraping the dish across the cement, trying to lap up every drop of gravy.

"I think you have just about cleaned the dish," I said and tickled him behind the ears. His tail began to wag and he clambered into my lap. "Let's go inside before it gets cold," I said as I picked up the dish. I hoisted him over my shoulder like a baby and carried him and the bowl into the house. I put Ollie into his basket and dropped the dish into the kitchen sink where Mother was washing up the supper dishes.

"Thank you," said Mother. "When we have done here, we can put up the boards on the windows before it gets dark. We don't want the warden banging on the door."

The wardens were men like Mr King, who because of age or infirmity could not go into the armed services, and some were women who had no children. They walked the streets at night and checked that no light was coming from any windows. If there was even a small chink of light showing, they knocked on the door and ordered that the windows be covered or the lights be turned off. There were no lights in the streets so everyone out after dark carried a flashlight with the light pointing downward. Even the trains ran without lights and the station names were removed. Many Londoners saw the night sky in all its glory for the first time in their lives.

I remember the day that a man wearing the uniform and tin helmet of a warden knocked on our door and asked for Helen. "She's at work," Mother told him.

"Right then, I'll have to ask you to give her these," he said, thrusting a paper package topped with a helmet into Mother's arms.

"What are these for?" Mother demanded.

The man explained that Helen was going to be a warden. Mother bristled. "But she's only a young girl," she stated trying to push the package back to him.

"No," the man replied, pushing the package back at her. "She is eighteen and old enough to be a warden. Please give her this uniform and helmet and tell her to come to the Town Hall on Wednesday evening at seven o'clock, for her duty roster. I don't make the rules. I'm only the messenger." Upon which, he turned on his heel and prepared to leave.

Mother glared after him. "All right, I'll give her the clothes but she is not going out if there is an air raid on," she cried, defiance in every word.

The man turned and gazed patiently at Mother. "Madam, your daughter will only have to go out if there *is* a warning of an air raid on. When there isn't an air raid on, she may stay at home with you in the air raid shelter, and listen to the bombs not falling on us from there."

Defeated, Mother slammed the door so hard the house shook. "Of all the impertinence," she muttered.

That evening, Mother emptied the washing-up water down the sink and dried her hands. "Right, let's get the window boards up." She stood on a chair and Helen and I handed the heavy boards up to her.

While we worked, we listened to the radio. The newscaster was talking about the enemy army's advance.

"Thank goodness for the English Channel," Mother muttered. "It isn't very wide but it looks as though the Germans are afraid of getting their feet wet." She fixed the last board in place. "There, that's done."

Mother climbed down from the chair she had been standing on and put it back at the table. "Go get your pyjamas and books or whatever you want to take to the shelter, Katie, and put my knitting with your stuff. I'll get my nightdress and the bedding and then I'll make the cocoa."

Quickly, I undressed and slipped into my pyjamas and dressing gown. I heard mother slowly climbing the stairs and going into her bedroom. I picked up my teddy bear from the bed and ran down to the kitchen. There I collected the books, paper, and pencils I wanted to take to the shelter. I put them in a bag with mother's knitting and put my coat on over my dressing gown. Mother came in carrying the rolled up bedding tied together with a length of rope.

"I wish I could leave this in the shelter," she sighed, "but then it would get damp and we would end up with pneumonia."

As Mother filled the electric kettle with water and switched it on, I went to the kitchen cupboard and took three hot water bottles from the hook on the wall. When the water in the kettle boiled, I handed the water bottles to mother, who carefully filled them and pushed them into the bundle of bedding. Then she set the kettle to boil again, and took a thermos jug and a tin of cocoa from the shelf. I closed my eyes and breathed deeply as the smell of cocoa filled the room for a few minutes before mother quickly screwed the stopper into the jug. She took her coat from a hook on the kitchen door and put it on. "Are you ready, Katie?"

"Yes Mummy." I picked up my flashlight and bag of books, pencils, paper, and Mother's knitting.

"Helen, come along. We're going to the shelter."

Helen came at a run stuffing her knitting into a bag, and struggling to get her arms into her coat. When this was accomplished she grinned and said, "Right, all present and correct. Come on Ollie."

Ollie struggled to his feet and followed us from the house. With the bundle of bedding over her shoulder and the thermos in her hand, mother struggled to turn out the lights and lock the door before following us down to the bottom of the garden.

I opened the shelter door. Ollie pushed inside and immediately snuggled into his blanket in the corner of the entryway. I stepped down into the shelter and Helen and mother followed me.

"Here we are," Mother said, dropping the bedding on the bunk that had been father's. She put the thermos beside three mugs on a wooden box and lit a candle. The light threw shadows on the walls. I was reminded of something. "Do you remember how Daddy used his hands to make animals appear on the wall?" I asked.

"Yes," said Mother with a sad smile. "Come on, let's get the bunks made up."

This did not take long and then mother poured the cocoa into the mugs. She handed one to me and one to Helen, and we sat on mother's bunk to drink. When the mugs were empty, Mother put them beside the entry to take to the house in the morning. Then she sat beside me and she and Helen began to knit. "Knitting socks for soldiers," was a slogan heard often on the radio. I wondered if the sailors and airmen had socks knitted for them.

I took out paper and pencil, and started to draw a picture. I drew father in his sailor uniform and Helen in her Warden jacket and helmet, Mummy, and myself. Then I drew Nellie, Lucy, Trot, and some guinea pigs. I surrounded them all with flowers.

Mother looked at the picture. "That's a lovely picture. Perhaps we can send it to Daddy."

"Yes," I said. "I do miss Daddy and Lucy and the guinea pigs, Mummy."

"I know sweetie. So do I. But now it's time to go to sleep. You have school in the morning."

I kissed Mother and wriggled into my bunk. Mother had put the hot water bottle at the top of the bed and I pushed it down to the bottom to keep my feet warm. The nights were beginning to get colder now but with luck, the water might stay warm until morning.

Sometime in the night, the siren went. I didn't hear it but Helen did and left to patrol the streets.

Chapter 4

When I woke in the morning, I felt for my flashlight under my pillow. Mother had already left the shelter. The cocoa jug, mugs, and mother's and Helen's bedding were gone too. I sat up and swung my legs out of the bunk. The dirt floor beneath an old piece of carpet was cold. Quickly, I slipped into my shoes. I put my coat on over my pyjamas and collecting my bedding, paper, pencils, and books, I climbed out of the shelter.

In the kitchen, Mother was making breakfast. She was mixing dried egg powder with water to make scrambled eggs. I liked scrambled powdered eggs, but mother said they did not taste like the real thing. Eggs were not rationed yet but sometimes the grocer did not have any. I could not remember when I had last eaten a banana or orange, and the ice-cream man never came round the street anymore. Every house in the street had fruit trees in the gardens and grew vegetables, so in spite of the small amounts of meat, butter, cheese, tea, and sugar that the shops could provide, no one went hungry.

"Morning sleepyhead," said Mother as she put a plate of egg in front of me. "Here you are. Eat up."

Ollie came and sat at my feet. I was not allowed to feed him at the table but sometimes I was careless and dropped something, "accidentally on purpose," Mother would say when she noticed. This morning, Ollie was lucky and he thanked me by licking my ankle.

Mother put bread and a jar of homemade jam on the table made from the berries from the garden. In September, the government had given families extra sugar for jam-making. When the flower beds were dug up, the berry bushes remained and I was allowed to feast on their fruit to my heart's content. I liked the blackberries the best, even though they were the hardest to pick. The strong thorns clutched at my clothes and left long scratches on my bare arms. The raspberries and loganberries were not quite as prickly and the red and black currants were the easiest to pick.

Whatever was left on the bushes when the extra sugar ration was distributed was picked, and for days, Mother stood over the stove stirring a pot of boiling berries and sugar. Her face turned red and sweat trickled down her neck. When she could stand the heat no longer, she opened the door to the garden. The sweet smell of sugar and fruit attracted wasps from miles around. They zoomed in like spitfires homing in on a German bomber. Mother put a saucer holding a spoonful of jam on the back door step to keep them happy and out of the house. This year Mother made twenty jars of jam.

"Have a slice of bread and jam and then get washed and dressed and get to school," she said, spreading a thin layer of jam on a piece of bread for herself. "I didn't hear a single plane last night so the school will still be there."

Ollie did not like jam and he returned despondently to his bed.

When I was ready to leave the house, Mother was putting on her coat. She worked during the mornings in the local re-housing office, trying to find places to stay for people whose homes had been bombed. She followed me out of the house, checking that I had my gas mask over my shoulder and my identity bracelet on my arm.

Mother gave me a hug and kissed me. "Have a safe day. See you later."

"You too Mummy."

Mother turned one way down the street and I went the other. As I passed the house next door, Jimmy and Dougie came running down the path.

We were puffing and red-faced by the time we skidded into the playground and managed to slide onto the end of the lines of children entering the school. Dougie went to his classroom and Jimmy and I went to ours.

"That was close," said Jimmy, as we hung our coats on the hooks along the wall. In the classroom, all the children sat in their seats until the teacher came in to the room. Then everyone stood up.

"Good morning, children," said the teacher.

"Good morning, Mrs Deane," we replied in unison.

Mrs Deane was very fat but had the thinnest ankles I had ever seen. *Just like a racehorse*, I thought. Secretly, I hoped that one day Mrs Deane would break one of them and have to stay at home. The older children called her the Dragon Lady. She always carried a ruler in her hand, and was quick to use it on the children's hands and legs if they stepped out of line. She also kept a cane in her desk drawer and, if that appeared, we knew someone was in serious trouble. I hated it when a child was caned.

"Sit down, children," Mrs Deane ordered. "When I say 'go,' take your gas masks from their boxes and put them on."

This was the first thing we did every morning now. Nobody thought that the enemy would gas us, but just in case, everyone carried their gas masks in a cardboard box around their necks. I hated wearing mine. It covered my whole face and smelled of rubber. It was held in place by stretchy rubber straps that caught and pulled my hair. The piece of the mask that filtered the gas stuck out the front like a snout. I thought it made us look like pigs.

After what seemed an eternity, the teacher removed her mask, and we could do the same. There followed wheezing and coughing until Mrs Deane said, "That's quite enough of that."

Miraculously everyone fell silent.

For the next twenty minutes, the whole class chanted the times tables.

"One two is two. Two twos are four. Three twos are six. Four twos are eight," all the way to, "twelve twelves are one hundred and forty four."

As we chanted, Mrs Deane walked around the room, up and down along the rows of desks. Every few minutes she bent over to listen to a child who, she suspected, was silently mouthing the words. When she could not hear anything, the ruler slapped down on the child's desk, making everyone jump. Mrs Deane bearing down on me was sure to clear every bit of knowledge from my head. When she asked the class a question, I never put up a hand to give an answer, for fear I gave the wrong one. I was more afraid of the Dragon Lady than the enemy bombs.

After the tables, Mrs Deane handed out sheets of paper on which a map of the British Isles was stencilled. The counties were indicated by thin lines. "Label all the counties and colour them different colours," Mrs Deane commanded.

We all bent to the task. I tried hard to keep the colours within the lines and prayed that I would not need to sharpen a pencil. The pencil sharpener was on Mrs Deane's desk, and she behaved as though it was her personal property. I felt guilty when I had to ask permission to use it.

At last the recess bell rang, and Mrs Deane put her ruler in her desk drawer. We did not move. Mrs Deane glared at each child, and when she was satisfied that we were all sitting absolutely still and silent, she said, "You may go. Quietly!"

Jimmy and I filed out and joined the line of children waiting for their recess bottle of milk. Each day, everyone was given a small bottle of milk. Mr Atkins, the headmaster, had told us that it was to make us grow strong. I just enjoyed the milk. When we had finished drinking, Jimmy and I put our empty bottles back in the crate and went to play. Jimmy went off to play ball with some of the boys and I found my girlfriends who were playing, "What's The Time Mr Fox?"

The rest of the morning was uneventful, and at lunchtime, I walked home with Jimmy and Dougie. Grandmother King was sitting in a chair in the front garden of the King's house. She had dozed off in the late-summer sunshine and her eye glasses had slipped down her nose. Jimmy and Dougie tiptoed past her.

"See you after lunch," Jimmy mouthed to me.

Mother was just putting two plates of salad on the table when I walked in.

"Ah, there you are. Did you have a good morning at school?"

"Same as usual. Mrs Deane shouted a lot. We were nearly late this morning."

"Oh dear. You'll have to leave earlier, or maybe not dawdle so much?"

"I s'pose. Where's Ollie?"

Although there was nothing in salad that Ollie liked, he normally sat beside me in the hope that something good would fall in his direction. Today he was not there.

"He went into the garden when I came home," said Mother. "I expect he has found a warm, sunny corner and fallen asleep."

Before returning to school, I went in search of Ollie. I found him where Mother said he might be; curled up in the sun in the glass-roofed veranda. I did not wake him.

I called goodbye to Mother as I ran past the door and on to the Kings' house. Grandmother King had gone from the garden, and as Jimmy and Dougie came out of the door, I heard her shouting goodbye to them from an upstairs room.

Mrs Deane's temper had not improved over lunch, but the warmth of the afternoon in the stuffy classroom slowed her down. When we returned from the afternoon recess, she told us to read our books. She sat at her desk and also opened a book.

After a few minutes, Jimmy leaned across and poked me. "The Dragon Lady's gone to sleep," he whispered.

I looked at Mrs Deane. She looked asleep. Certainly her eyes were closed. A large bluebottle fly buzzed around the room. It flew around the teacher's desk. Now all the children were watching Mrs Deane and the fly. Closer and closer, the fly circled around her head like a plane circling a landing strip. We all held our breath. Suddenly the fly stopped buzzing. Very gently it landed on her nose!

Mrs Deane bolted upright and swatted at the tickle. The fly buzzed indignantly and flew out of reach. A few children giggled and Mrs Deane glared them into silence. "What's so funny? Get on with your reading," she yelled.

Heads bent obediently over the books but every child was grinning.

Within minutes of afternoon dismissal, everyone in the school had heard about The Dragon Lady and the fly. Jimmy, Dougie, and I skipped all the way home.

I said goodbye to Jimmy and Dougie at their gate and rushed into the house eager to tell Mother about the fly. "Do you know what happened..."

I stopped in mid-sentence. Mother was sitting at the table crying. I ran to her.

"Mummy. What's wrong?"

Mother put her arms around me and held me tight. "It's Ollie," she gulped. "When he didn't come in, I went out to find him. I thought he was sleeping but when I touched him and said his name he didn't move. I'm sorry. He was dead."

I could not believe what Mother had said. "No, he can't be. He *was* sleeping."

"No, Katie, he must have died in his sleep. You know he was very old. Perhaps it was a good thing. He wouldn't have been happy when he lost his sight and hearing completely."

I clung to Mother and we both wept. Why was everything dying? When there were no more tears to shed I asked, "Where is he?"

"I've laid him in his kennel blanket and put him in a cardboard carton. It's in the greenhouse. Now that you are here we will bury him in the garden. We can put his ball in with him if you like."

I nodded and went to fetch the hairless tennis ball that Ollie loved to chase. Mother took my hand and we walked down the garden to the greenhouse. I looked in the carton. Ollie was still curled up as though sleeping. I stroked him in his favourite spot behind the ears and placed the ball by his side.

Mother closed the carton and picked it up. "I thought we could put him under the rose bush with Lucy. They'll be together again," she said.

I nodded. Mother had already prepared a hole. Gently, she placed the carton in the earth. She picked up a handful of soil and dropped it onto the carton. "Goodbye Ollie, we will miss you."

I did the same. I could not speak and tears rolled down my cheeks. Mother shovelled earth into the hole, and marked the spot with a small, wooden cross she had made from two twigs. I pulled the petals from a full-blown rose and dropped them onto the little grave.

Mother and I were very quiet for the rest of the day. When Helen came home, we told her about Ollie and she held us both in a hug. "Perhaps it is a good thing. He would have been very sad when he could no longer see or hear us," she said.

Supper was not the same without Ollie sitting at my feet. That night, we walked to the shelter in silence. When I saw Ollie's shelter blanket inside the shelter door, I felt the tears begin to fall again. Mother quickly picked the blanket up and tucked it under her bunk. I got straight into my bunk when it was made up and watched while mother wrote a letter to father, telling him of Ollie's death. Then she climbed into my bunk and held me as I cried myself to sleep.

The next day was Saturday and I was eating my breakfast when someone knocked on the front door. Mother went to see who it was. I heard the door open and mother say, "Come in." I swallowed my last bite of toast and hurried to see who had come to visit. Jimmy and Dougie's father Mr King was standing in the hall talking to mother, who turned to me.

"Katie, Mr King has come to ask if you would like to go with him and the boys to see the barrage balloons being sent up," she said.

"Yes please, Mr King. Thank you."

"Good. Be ready at nine o'clock. Wear your raincoat, in case it rains, and bring your gas mask. Mrs King will make some sandwiches for our lunch."

I ran upstairs to brush my teeth. Then I combed my hair and put on my identification bracelet. I was not worried that we would be caught in an air raid, but I knew mother would not let me go on the train without it.

At nine o'clock, I was ready and waiting at the gate for Mr King, Dougie, and Jimmy. My gas mask, in its small cardboard box, was slung over my head and shoulder. Mother gave me last-minute instructions.

"Stay close to Mr King and behave yourself. And thank Mr King when you get home."

"I will."

The Kings' door opened and Dougie and Jimmy ran out and rushed to join me. Mr King was saying goodbye to Mrs King and the boys' grandmother. He came to the gate of our house and stopped to speak to Mother.

"I'll bring Katie home safely. Don't worry," he said.

"I'm sure you will," mother said. "Thank you very much for thinking of Katie. It will take her mind off Ollie."

Mr King nodded. Jimmy had told him about Ollie's death.

"Right," he said to us. "Let's get going." Mother waved goodbye as we skipped ahead of Mr King along the street.

At the end of the road, Mr King gathered us to him and we walked together to the Underground station. The boys and I did not ride the tube train often and we were eager to begin the trip. Mr King bought tickets and gave one to each of us. I felt very grown-up as I handed my ticket to the man guarding the entry to the trains. We rode the moving stairs down to the platform. The train ran on track that was laid two or three feet lower than the platform. Mr King told us that we must stay back from the edge of the platform because the track was electrified and if we fell on it, we would be burned. Dougie saw a little mouse running along the track.

"How come he doesn't get burned, Daddy?" he asked.

"Because to complete the electrical circuit that would send electricity through his body he must touch the electrified line and the ground at the same time. The mouse's legs are too short for him to do that," Mr King explained.

We thought about that for a minute. Then Jimmy said, "So if I could balance on the electrified line, I wouldn't be burned?"

Mr King laughed. "I suppose not." Then very seriously he added, "But don't you dare think of trying it!"

Suddenly, the track seemed to be humming and a low rumbling noise travelled towards us from the darkness of the tunnel. The rumbling grew louder until, with a loud whoosh and clatter, a train roared into the station and screeched to a halt. Doors along the length of the train opened and we all climbed into the nearest carriage. There were already many people on board and there were no more seats to be had. Mr King put the three of us against the end seat and stood in front of us, holding onto a strap above his head.

As the train got closer to the centre of London, we saw people carrying blankets and pillows off the platforms. Mr King explained that they slept on the platforms because they did not have air raid shelters.

At every stop, a few people left the train but a larger number got on. I found myself nose to coat button with Mr King. I tried to move but was hemmed in on either side by the boys, who were also being crushed into other passengers. I managed to turn my head but then the button was pressed into my cheek. I was relieved when Mr King said, "We get off at the next station. Get ready to push your way through the crowd on the platform. Stay close behind me. Jimmy you hold onto my coat, Katie hold Jimmy's hand, and Dougie, you hold Katie's other hand."

The train squealed to a stop at the next station and as soon as the doors opened, Mr King stepped out, with us hanging on behind him. This station was so deep underground that it took two moving staircases to reach ground level. I was happy to breathe fresh air again after being crushed against so many bodies.

I soon realized that there were as many people in the streets as there had been in the trains. Men and women in uniform, young women pushing babies in prams, and older women holding onto walking children, crowded the pavement, while more zigzagged across the road between the buses, bicycles, ambulances, and a few cabs. It was noisier too. Old men and young boys selling newspapers were shouting out the headlines. Conductors on the buses were shouting at people trying to board, that there was, "No more room." Pedestrians called out to the few passing cabs, and cyclists rang their bicycle bells at pedestrians wandering across the road.

Mr King suggested that everyone hold hands and he took me in one hand and Dougie in the other. Jimmy held tightly onto Dougie's other hand. In this way, we made our way to the park where the balloons were to be launched.

Barrage balloons were sent up into the skies to try to interfere with the enemy planes. The deflated balloons lay on concrete pads. Thick metal cables attached them to winches on the back of trucks. Young women in uniform were running around, checking the balloons, and manning the winches. A few minutes after we arrived, the winch on one of the trucks began to turn.

As the balloon grew, we could see thinner lines running from its sides to the concrete pad. Mr King explained that when a balloon was fully inflated, it was as tall as a house and more than twice that in length. We watched wide-eyed as the balloon grew larger and larger. It became egg-shaped with large, ear-like fins at the narrower end. "Stabilizers" explained Mr King.

A young man in the uniform of an airman was standing beside Dougie. He leaned down and whispered in Dougie's ear. Dougie giggled and whispered to Jimmy. I poked Jimmy and he said, "That man said they look like Mickey Mouse ears."

Several of the women were now untying the cords that were holding the balloon down, and it began to rise into the air. All three of us were jumping up and down and shouting encouragement as the balloon rose higher and higher until it was bobbing about in the clouds, but still attached to the truck by a long, metal cord.

One by one all the balloons were inflated and guided into the sky. As the last one settled into place, the man beside Dougie gazed upward and said, "I don't know why they don't cut the strings on them and let this little island sink into the sea."

We looked at him in horror. "That's not a very nice thing to say," I said.

The man laughed and said, "I was joking. I'm from Canada and that country is big. If you dropped this country onto the Canadian Prairies, it would disappear in the wheat fields. I'm used to wide-open spaces and never-ending skies. You'd need thousands of those balloons to fill our skies."

Mr King grinned. "Perhaps it's just as well we are a small island. We'd never find enough material to make that many balloons. My mother used to tell me that good things come in small parcels, so don't write us off yet. We are not going to give in to a bully."

"I believe you. I wouldn't be here if I didn't. I'm a pilot so I know these things are doing a good job."

"We're gonna have a picnic," said Dougie. "If you like, I can share my sandwiches with you."

The airman looked at his watch. "Thanks, that's real nice of you, but I have to go now. I'm billeted with a lovely lady who will be very annoyed if I miss the lunch she's making for me." He turned to Jimmy, me, and Dougie and putting his hand in his pocket, he pulled out three thin strips of something wrapped in paper. "Here you are," he said, handing one to each of us. "This is gum. Eat it after your picnic, but don't swallow it. Have a safe journey home."

We all said thank you, but were not sure what we had been given.

The airman shook Mr King's hand. "Take care," he said. "You too," said Mr King. "Thank you for coming to help us. May God protect you."

The Canadian nodded and patted Mr King on the back as he walked away. "Goodbye kids."

"Goodbye," we chorused.

"Right," said Mr King. "Let's find a bench to sit on and eat and then we must go home. We don't want to be late and have our mothers worrying about us."

We found a bench beneath a large oak tree and Mr King handed round the sandwiches; large slabs of bread stuck together with a thin spreading of fish paste, and apples from the trees in the Kings' garden. We ate hungrily, carefully picking up the crumbs. Mr King poured some weak, milky tea into cups for everyone, collected the sandwich wrappings and apple cores and took them to a waste bin a few yards down the path.

Dougie remembered the gum that the airman had given us. He pulled his piece from his pocket and carefully unwrapped it. Jimmy and I followed suit. We all three stared at the thin, pink strips. We had never had gum before and were not sure what to do with it.

"The man said eat it," said Jimmy.

"But don't swallow it," I warned.

Dougie popped his gum into his mouth and began to chew. Jimmy and I watched to see if he liked it. Dougie said nothing.

"Well," said Jimmy impatiently. "Is it good?"

Dougie grimaced. "It's sort of like rubber. But it tastes good. Like a peppermint."

Jimmy put his gum in his mouth and after watching his face, I popped my piece into mine. We all chewed for several minutes and then Dougie said, "It doesn't taste like anything now. What do I do with it?"

"Don't swallow it," I warned again. The gum was sticking to my teeth and I thought it might stick to the inside of my stomach if I swallowed it.

Mr King returned and said, "Are you ready to go home?"

"Daddy, what can we do with the gum the airman gave us? It doesn't taste good anymore."

"Have you got the paper it was wrapped in?"

Dougie fished in his pocket and brought out the crumpled wrapping.

"Good," said Mr King. "Take the gum out of your mouth and put it in the paper. You two do the same," he said to Jimmy and me. "Come along. I'll drop these in the waste bin at the park gate."

It was getting dark by the time we reached the station. People were already beginning to claim a spot to sleep on the platforms. Babies were crying and tired, and mothers were trying to keep small children close to them. One little group was playing cards and further along, a man was playing tunes on a mouth organ to some older children. A couple of the girls started to dance and a few of the adults sang along with the music. I thought of my mother at home. She would be putting the boards up on the windows, and thinking about what to have for tea. I was glad that we had our own shelter to sleep in, but thought that it might be nice to spend a night here just once. The children were enjoying the music and it was lonely sometimes in the shelter with Mother and Helen. We would not even have Ollie to keep us company now.

A train rumbled and roared out of the tunnel and alongside the platform. When it stopped and the doors opened, Mr King herded us on to it. This time, we managed to find seats. Mr King pulled Dougie onto his knees so that a lady could sit down. It was very hot and stuffy in the train and we were feeling tired. It was not long before Dougie fell asleep. Jimmy and I nudged one another and grinned at Dougie. The train rattled through the dark tunnels and the next thing I knew, Mr King was gently shaking me and saying, "We get off at the next stop, Katie."

Chapter 5

The planes were dropping bombs on London day and night. Sometimes, in the daytime, we could see *our* planes, the Spitfires, dipping and diving at the bombers in the sky. We never dawdled on the way to school now that it was cold in the mornings. Mrs Deane was grumpier than ever because the school was not as warm as she would have liked. The dark nights meant that more planes came across the Channel and dropped their bombs so that sometimes it was hard to sleep.

There were air raid shelters in the school field, and when the warning sounded the teachers took the children into them. On one particularly dull day in late October, the air raid warning went off during morning school.

Mrs Deane shouted, "Make sure you have your gas masks and line up behind me."

Outside the school, children were being organized into lines and marched toward the shelters. The teachers were running around like ants but the children were enjoying the break in routine. Jimmy and I chatted happily as we marched along and filed into the shelters. These were large, rectangular, brick buildings with benches down the walls inside. I kept close to the child ahead of me and sat down, leaving a space for Jimmy to sit beside me. Everyone was scrunched up tightly to his or her neighbour while the teachers stood in the aisle trying to call out names. I listened carefully for my name to be called because the Dragon Lady got annoyed when she had to say a name twice.

When everyone was accounted for, Mrs Deane decided that her class should make good use of the time by practising the gas mask drill. Everyone groaned, Jimmy the loudest.

"That's enough of that, Jimmy King. You may be glad you have a gas mask one day. Now on the count of three, open your boxes, remove your gas masks and put them on. ONE, TWO, THREE."

In the cramped shelter, it was not easy to get the masks on. Squeals and cries of "Mind what 'yer doin,'" echoed round the shelter as elbows were stuck in neighbours' ribs. Once the masks were on our heads, the snout-like air filters crashed together as children turned to speak to one another. Soon we were all giggling and purposely banging our masks together.

Someone began snorting like a pig, and then everyone was doing it. I could see that Mrs Deane was getting annoyed, and without a ruler to slap on a desk, she lashed out with her hand at anything she could hit. This happened to be Jimmy's head, but he ducked just as Mrs Deane was about to make contact. She hit the wall instead.

The sound of hand meeting cement resounded the length of the shelter and everyone fell silent. We all watched in horror as Mrs Deane looked at her hand. It was hanging at a strange angle. At that moment, the all-clear sounded and Miss Long, Dougie's teacher, began to usher the children out of the door. When Jimmy and I reached the school, we looked back and saw Miss Long helping Mrs Deane across the playground. Mrs Deane was holding her arm across her body and she looked very pale.

Back in the classroom, the children removed the gas masks and put them in their boxes. We sat at our desks wondering what would happen next.

After a few minutes, the headmaster, Mr Atkins, came into the room.

"Mrs Deane has broken her wrist and has gone to the hospital," he announced. "You can all go home now and don't come back until tomorrow morning."

Outside, several boys slapped Jimmy on the back. "Thanks Jimmy. You should duck more often," Andy Jakes called as he ran past.

Jimmy did not look very happy. "I'm really gonna get it when Mrs Deane comes back," he sighed.

"She shouldn't have tried to hit you," I said. "Cheer up. Bring your model planes into my house this afternoon and we'll play at dogfights."

Chapter 6

I was dreaming. I was running with Ollie through a meadow filled with flowers. Suddenly, a swarm of bees was buzzing around my head. I tried to outrun it but I could not. My legs felt heavy as lead. There was a loud clap of thunder and the ground lurched. I fell down and the bees dropped like stones around my head. The noise woke me. I sat up with a start and by the light from my mother's flashlight, I saw Mother sitting up in her bunk listening to the noise. She was pulling on her coat. I realized that I could still hear stones dropping. Something was falling on the roof of the shelter above my head. When it stopped, mother climbed out of the shelter.

I found my flashlight and slipped out of my bunk. I put on my shoes, and as I followed her outside, I heard her say, "Oh my God."

Beams from searchlights searched for the enemy plane, crisscrossing the sky while the guns on the heath fired, trying to bring the plane down. Mother was staring at the Kings' house. I followed her gaze and found myself looking into the upstairs bedrooms. The back of the house had collapsed into the garden.

Mother started to run toward the street and I followed her. We found Mrs King with Jimmy and Dougie clinging to her. They were standing in the middle of the road looking lost and dazed. Mother put her arm around Mrs King.

"Where's your mother?" she asked.

"Upstairs," Mrs King whispered.

To our relief the All Clear siren began to wail and neighbours from the other houses came into the street gathering in a circle around us. Mr King came running down the street. He was on duty and had come as soon as he heard the bomb fall. He ran into the house and several minutes later, came out alone.

"Mother's alive," he said, "but I don't want to move her. She may be injured. She is sitting on the bed with her feet dangling in space. The ambulance will be here immediately."

As he spoke, the sound of a clanging bell reached us and the crowd opened up to let the ambulance through. Mr King spoke to the attendants and led them into the house. The people in the street were silent. I looked at Jimmy and Dougie. Their eyes were wide open, but they did not seem to see anything. They were shivering in their pyjamas and I noticed that they had nothing on their feet. Helen had come running along the street and she knelt down, trying to comfort them.

Several minutes passed before Mr King and the attendants came out of the house, carrying Jimmy and Dougie's grandmother on a stretcher. While they put the stretcher into the ambulance, Mr King ran over to Mrs King.

"I'm going to the hospital," he said.

Mother put her hand on Mrs King's shoulder. "You go too," she said. "There's no more danger. I'll take the boys into my house until you get back." Mother pushed Mrs King toward the ambulance as the crowd that had gathered began to move silently back to their homes.

Mother took the boys' hands in hers and the ambulance pulled away. "Come along," she said, "I'll make some cocoa and then you can sleep in my bed. Helen, Katie, run ahead please, and get some blankets from the cupboard upstairs."

When we came down with the blankets, we found that Mother had relit the fire in the living room and the boys were sitting in front of it. Now she was making cocoa.

Helen took mugs from the cupboard.

"Put the blankets round Jimmy and Dougie, Katie. The cocoa's nearly ready."

I hurried to do as I was told. I was frightened by the way the boys looked. Their eyes were saucers in their grey faces and they were still shivering.

Mother came in from the kitchen with five steaming mugs of cocoa on a tray.

"Here we are," she said brightly. "This will make you feel better. It's hot so be careful when you drink."

Jimmy and Dougie took the mugs and stared into them as though they had never seen cocoa before. I sat beside them and sipped from my mug. The cocoa was very sweet. "It's very good," I said to Jimmy.

Jimmy looked at me and then to the mug he was holding. I took another sip from my mug. Jimmy nodded and copied me. He nudged Dougie. "Drink your cocoa, Dougie."

Dougie started as though woken from sleep and carefully holding the mug with both hands put it to his lips. As the sweet, warm cocoa filled their tummies, the boys' colour began to lose the dreadful grey-ness and the shivering stopped.

When the mugs were empty, mother took them away and said, "Let's go upstairs and try to sleep shall we?" The boys clutched their blankets around them. Mother took Dougie's hand. Helen picked up Jimmy and followed Mother up the stairs to her bedroom. She kissed Jimmy's forehead and laid him gently in mother's bed. "Do you need any help?" she asked.

"No thank you Helen," mother said. "You've done your bit as warden tonight. You get to bed, you have to go to work tomorrow." Mother gave Dougie a hug and helped him onto the bed beside Jimmy. She turned to me and said, "You get in beside them, Katie."

She tucked me in and kissed me goodnight. Jimmy was staring into the dimly lit room, clutching the bedclothes tightly. Tears slid down his cheeks. Mother gently wiped them away. She lay down beside him and took one of his hands in hers. "The nasty plane has gone back to its own country now, Jimmy. I'll stay here beside you and keep you safe. Close your eyes, there's a good boy. You'll feel better if you go to sleep."

I listened until fright and exhaustion lured the boys into sleep and then I whispered across them to Mother. "Will their grandma be all right, Mummy?"

"I hope so, sweetie, but I don't know. Pray for her."

I closed my eyes and said a prayer in my head. *Dear God, please make Jimmy's grandmother better and keep us all safe. And keep Daddy safe so he can come home to Mummy, Helen, and me. And look after Lucy and Ollie now that they are with you and if you can, give Ollie some meat sometimes because he does like meat and he hasn't had any for a long time. Thank you God. Amen.*

I was wakened the next morning by a drop of cold water falling on my nose. I opened my eyes in surprise and saw that a crack had appeared in the ceiling above my head. Water was seeping through it. I leapt out of bed before the next drop fell. Jimmy and Dougie were still asleep out of the range of the leak.

I slipped into my slippers and ran out of the bedroom, colliding with mother who was coming up the stairs carrying pails and bowls.

"Oh good, you're awake," she said. "Helen has gone to work. Here, take some of these bowls and put them under any leaks you can find. The bomb blast must have blown some of the tiles off the roof, and it is raining cats and dogs this morning."

I realized that there were sounds of dripping water coming from all the rooms.

"I'll put a bowl on the bed," I said. "The water is dripping on it but Jimmy and Dougie are still asleep in the dry."

The water made more noise dripping into the pails and bowls than it did dripping onto the floor and bedclothes, but it did not wake the boys. When all the drips had been dealt with, mother and I went downstairs.

"We'll have to keep an eye on the pails and bowls and empty them regularly if this rain keeps up," said mother. "I'm afraid the bomb also broke all the glass in the veranda and a load of bricks and slates are scattered over the garden. But look on the bright side. The house is still standing and most of the windowpanes are still in place. I think you had better stay at home today. I am going to need your help cleaning up the mess."

Mother took the toasting fork from the cupboard drawer and handed it to me. "The fire's lit so will you please make some toast for breakfast? The boys will probably wake up soon."

Mother was right and I was still toasting bread at the fire when Jimmy and Dougie crept into the kitchen. Mother hugged them and sat them at the table. She took the bread I had toasted and spread it with jam. "Here you go boys. You'll have to eat in your pyjamas this morning. When your mummy comes home I expect she'll be able to go into the house to get you some clothes to wear."

We were eating when the doorbell rang and mother got up to open the door. I followed her to the hallway. Mr and Mrs King stood on the doorstep. "Come in, come in," said Mother. "How's your mother?"

Before she was answered, mother realized that the news was bad. Mrs King dissolved into tears and Mr King put his arm around her. "I'm afraid she didn't make it," he said.

"Oh, I am so sorry. Come into the kitchen. The boys are there having some breakfast. I'll take Katie out and you can spend time with them alone."

She saw me standing in the doorway and took my hand. Mr and Mrs King went into the kitchen. Mother closed the door and led me to the stairs where we sat down.

"What's happened?" I asked. "What didn't their grandma make?"

Mother pulled me onto her lap. "Their grandma has died."

I was puzzled and angry. "But I asked God to make her better."

"I know. I prayed to him too. I suppose that sometimes God can't answer our prayers."

I sat silently thinking. "Why do the planes drop bombs on us?" I asked.

"Because a silly little man in Europe thinks he should be able to make everyone do what he wants them to do."

I stood up and stamped my foot. "I hate that man. I hate him, I hate him, I hate him." I ran up the stairs and threw myself onto my bed. What had Jimmy's grandmother done that God would let her die? And why should he punish Jimmy and Dougie? It wasn't Dougie's fault that the Dragon Lady had broken her wrist. It was that little man in Europe's fault. It was because of him that Daddy was not with us. Nothing was fair. I lay staring at the cracks in the ceiling and feeling mad at God and that little man in Europe. It was all his fault.

After a while, I heard Mr and Mrs King talking to Mother in the hallway. Then the front door opened and closed and I heard Mother going into the kitchen. I got up and went to look out of the window. I could see the broken glass and pieces of brick lying on the veranda floor and bricks and tiles scattered among the vegetables. There were some bricks in the water in the pond and I wondered if the fish were all right. The sky was as grey as my thoughts and the rain fell relent-lessly. I went back to my bed and listened to the water plopping into the bucket in the middle of the room. The whole ceiling was covered in cracks.

I began using the cracks as a maze, trying to get from one side of the ceiling to the other without coming to a dead end.

The doorbell rang again and I heard mother opening the door to let Mrs King in. I went to the top of the stairs and looked down into the hall. Mrs King was carrying clothes and shoes for Jimmy and Dougie. She went into the living room and closed the door.

Mother looked up the stairs. "Come down Katie. Jimmy and Dougie are going in a few minutes. You had better say goodbye to them because you may not see them again."

I ran down the stairs as Mrs King and the boys came into the hall.

"You're sure you are going to be all right?" Mother asked Mrs King.

"Yes thank you. We are going to stay with my sister until we can move into another house. You've been very kind. I hope all goes well with you."

I went over to the boys. "Mummy says you're going away," I said. Dougie nodded.

"I'm sorry about your grandma, Jimmy, and I'm sorry you are not going to be next door any more. I'll miss you both."

"Yeah, I'll miss you too. Goodbye."

"Goodbye, Jimmy. Goodbye, Dougie."

Mrs King gathered the boys to her. "Come along, Daddy's waiting for us." She gave Mother a hug and hurried to the street where Mr King stood beside a taxi. They all climbed into the cab and waved goodbye. I watched as they were driven into the rain and out of my life. There was one good thing, I decided. Jimmy would not have to see Mrs Deane again.

Mother closed the door. "Right, Katie. Let's check the buckets and bowls and hope it stops raining before we have a flood."

Between emptying pails, Mother and I swept up glass and cleared the bricks and tiles from the garden and the pond. The glass in the windows at the back of the house and the glass in the veranda had been blown out. My father had served in India after the First World War ended and had seen verandas on the houses there. When he married and bought our house, he put a veranda on the back wall. It was an open porch that ran the width of the house and had a glass roof. Most of the glass was now on the porch, the lawn, and in the pond, along with bricks and slates from the Kings' house.

The fish were still swimming around in the rain but I could not find Trot, my tortoise. She had been sleeping out the winter in her box in the veranda, but I could not see the box. A large piece of wall from the Kings' house had fallen in our garden. It was under this that I found her. Her box was smashed and her shell was badly cracked. I picked her up and ran to Mother.

"Mummy, Mummy, Trot is hurt."

Mother took her and looked inside the shell quietly calling, "Trot, Trot."

Trot did not put her head out and her legs hung limply from her shell.

"I am sorry, Katie. Trot has died. We'll have to put her with Lucy and Ollie."

My legs felt like jelly and I collapsed to the ground. I put my head in my hands and howled. Mother knelt down and took me in her arms. She did not say anything. She just let me cry. When I could speak I asked her, "Why did the bomb have to kill Trot? She never hurt anyone."

Mother hugged me closer. "I don't know, Katie. I wish I could stop this war but I can't. Come along and we will put Trot with Lucy and Ollie. They will look after her."

It was evening before the rain stopped. The clouds swept away, leaving a clear, star-studded sky. Mother and I emptied the last pail and bowl before collecting up the night-time supplies and heading for the shelter. Helen was on warden duty and would not come home until the raids ended.

Mother and I had just settled ourselves for sleep when the air raid siren sounded. Before long, we heard the thump, thump of the enemy planes' engines. The guns on the ground opened fire and added to the whine of bombs falling. Mother climbed into my bunk and pulled me close. She pulled the blankets over our heads to muffle the noise. Snuggled together and exhausted from the struggles and sadness of the day, Mother and I fell asleep to a lullaby of planes and bombs and guns.

The next morning dawned clear and frosty. I woke to silence and a small sliver of daylight peeking around the edge of the shelter door. Mother and Helen had already gone. It must be getting late. I hurried into my clothes and coat and ran up to the house. Mother was cooking powdered eggs again. Good.

"Morning Katie. Your breakfast is ready. You'll have to be quick. We slept in late."

Eggs eaten, teeth and hair brushed, I was ready for school.

Mother kissed me goodbye at the gate. She pushed a note into my coat pocket.

"Give that to Mrs Deane. It's to tell her why you were not in school yesterday. I'll see you at lunchtime."

When I reached the school, the children in the schoolyard were very excited. Mary Smith ran over to me. She was jumping up and down.

"Guess what. Some bombs fell on the school last night. Incendries or something. They started fires in the hallways."

"Are we having a day off?" I asked hopefully.

"Nah. The classrooms are all right," Mary scoffed.

The bell rang and the children filed into school. They hung their coats on the pegs in the hall where there was a strong smell of burnt paint. As he hung up his coat, one boy noticed that the paint on the walls had blistered. He pressed a blister with his thumb and it popped open.

"Hey this is fun," he said. Soon all the children were happily popping the paint blisters.

"Stop that at once," said a loud voice.

We froze where we were. Dragon Lady was standing in the doorway. Her right wrist was encased in a plaster cast and she was holding her ruler in her left hand.

"She can't hit as hard with her left hand," the boy beside me whispered.

"Good, serves her right," I whispered back.

"Get into the classroom and stand by your desks," Mrs Deane bellowed.

We quietly filed into our rooms.

There were a few empty desks already in the class. They had belonged to children whose homes had been bombed and they had moved away, or to some who were still living in the countryside, and a few who had gone to live with relatives in Canada and the U.S.A. From today, Jimmy's desk would be empty. We had sat beside one another since our first day in school and looking at the empty desk, I felt empty too.

I remembered the note in my coat pocket and raised my hand.

"Yes," said Mrs Deane.

"Please Mrs Deane, I have a note for you in my coat pocket. Can I go and fetch it?"

"I am sure, Katie, that you are perfectly capable of going to get something from your coat pocket. What should you have said? "

I had not the faintest idea.

"I ... I don't know," I stammered. I felt my face going red.

Mrs Deane's ruler rapped on the desk.

"I am tired of trying to teach children who do not listen to me," she complained. "What you should have said, Katie, is, '*May* I go and fetch it?'"

"Yes, Mrs Deane. May I go to fetch the note?"

"Yes, you may. And come straight back."

When I returned, Mrs Deane was taking attendance. I put the note on her desk and sat down. When she finished the roll call, she picked up the note. Looking over the top of the paper at me, she asked, "You live next door to Jimmy King, do you?"

"Yes, Mrs Deane."

"Was it Jimmy's home that was bombed?"

"Yes, Mrs Deane."

"Is Jimmy all right?"

"Yes, but his grandma died."

"I am sorry to hear that. Do you know if he will be coming back to school?"

"I don't think so. Mr and Mrs King and Jimmy and his brother have gone to live with his aunt, until they find somewhere else to live."

"Thank you, Katie. If you hear where they are living, let me know. I should like to send my condolences."

I wondered what 'condolences' were. Mrs Deane sounded as though she really was sorry about Jimmy's grandmother. Perhaps she was not all bad.

At recess we were treated to another bit of excitement. During the night, the temperature had gone below freezing . When we went out at recess, we found that the milk had frozen in the bottles. Each bottle had a little cardboard-capped column of frozen milk sticking out of its neck. We all removed the cardboard caps and sucked the frozen milk like ice-lollies. Mrs Deane turned the event into a science lesson, explaining that the cold had caused the bottles to shrink and squeeze out the milk when it froze.

At lunchtime, I got home to find a man mending the holes in the roof. Mother explained that when he had finished on the roof, he would board up the broken window panes until he could get some glass.

"Daddy will have to mend the cracks in the ceiling when he comes home. With the holes in the roof mended, the rain won't get into the attic and drip through the cracks," Mother explained.

Before I returned to school, I went out to watch the man on the roof. I wished I could get on the roof with him. I would probably be able to see the school from up there. The man climbed down and began boarding up the windows at the back of the house. The ones at the front had not been damaged by the blast. He held the nails he was using between his lips, the way my mother held pins in her mouth when she was laying a paper pattern on material before cutting it out. *If I put pins in my mouth,* I thought, *mother would be very cross with me.* Why were there so many things grown-ups could do and children could not I wondered. It was very unfair!

There was no air raid that night and mother, Helen, and I enjoyed a deep sleep. The next morning, as we walked together to the house, mother stopped at the pond and stared at the water. "I think the water is lower than usual," she said. "We'll have to keep an eye on it."

At lunchtime, I ran to the garden to check the water level in the pond. What I saw sent me running back to the house shouting, "Mummy, Mummy, there is only a tiny drop of water in the pond and the fish are flopping about in it!"

Mother came running out. Sure enough, there was a small puddle of water in the deepest part of the pond and it was filled with writhing bodies of goldfish, gasping in the air.

"Quick, Katie go and bring out the biggest saucepan you can find in the kitchen. I'll use a pail and we'll fill the pond with water from the rain barrel."

While I was fetching a saucepan from the house, mother threw several pails of rainwater into the pond. The large fish immediately spread out and recovered. Soon the pond was half-filled with water, but the rain barrel was almost empty.

"That bomb falling has cracked the cement of the pond. The rain yesterday kept it filled but we can't expect that to happen every day," said mother. "I'm afraid the pond will empty again tomorrow unless we get rain."

"Then we'll have to keep filling it from the tap," I said.

"No we can't do that."

"Why not?"

"Because we're not supposed to use the tap water unnecessarily. The firemen need it to fight the fires caused by the bombs."

"What will happen to the fish then?"

"I'm afraid they will die. They are too big to put in an aquarium." I burst into tears. This was too much. Mother held me close. She was near to tears herself. "Come on Katie, don't cry. We've still got one another," she said. "Perhaps the fish will keep Ollie company and give Lucy something to watch."

I wiped the tears away with my hand. Mother was right. We still had one another and when the war ended, Father would come home.

Chapter 7

1941 NEW NEIGHBOURS AND A NEW PET

Where the Kings' house had stood, there was now an empty piece of ground. Men had come and pulled down the part of the house that was still standing and taken everything away. Mother said they could use the bricks and doors to build something else.

The planes were still dropping bombs on London all the time, but the year started with something good happening. A house across the street became empty when the old lady who lived there went to live with her daughter in the countryside. Almost immediately, a new family moved in. They were Mr and Mrs Davis, and their two children, Vicky and Violet. They had been bombed out of their house in the east end of London.

Vicky was almost eight years old like me, and we became friends straight away. Violet was still too young to go to school. It was nice to have someone to walk to and from school with again. I wondered if Jimmy and Dougie had found new friends.

I spent a lot of time playing at Vicky's house. Because there was a young child in the family, Mrs Davis did not have to go to work. This meant that there was always someone at home when Vicky and I came home from school in the afternoon. Married women with school-age children often worked in the munitions factories and many children came home to empty houses or to older siblings or neighbours who kept an eye on them. The Davises had an indoor, air raid shelter. I had never seen one like it before. It was a large cage with a metal floor and roof and metal mesh all around the sides. It made a good cage for playing animals at the zoo. Vicky, Violet, and I would take turns climbing in and pretending to be lions and tigers or monkeys, or any other animal we thought of. Mr Davis worked in a factory at night so we had to do our roaring and chattering very quietly so he could sleep in the daytime.

So many houses had been bombed that the number of people needing somewhere to live had increased. Mother was working full-time now in the Council Housing Office, and she decided to find someone to help with the housework. Through her work, she had met a lady who was too old to have to work but wanted to earn a little bit of pocket money for herself. Her name was Mrs Smithers and Mother had found her a room in someone's home when her own house was bombed.

Mrs Smithers was a widow, a true Cockney, born within the sound of Bow Bells, and cheeky as a London sparrow. Small and thin, she exuded energy; a perpetual motion machine whizzing round the house, brandishing the vacuum cleaner at breakneck speed, and singing at the top of her lungs. I never knew what colour her hair was because it was always hidden beneath a flowered scarf wound around her head, and kept in place by a tiny bow on her forehead. It seemed that nothing could bring her down. Her home in the East End lay in ruins, her only son was somewhere in a tank in the Egyptian desert, and she was living in one room in a stranger's home. Yet she always arrived with a smile on her face, and a new idea of what we should do to Adolf Hitler when we caught him. Not for one moment did she believe that he would not be caught and that the British would not be victorious. Her hero was Winston Churchill. "'E won't let them Germans into London," she proudly stated.

She came to the house once a week on Wednesdays, arriving before mother and I left the house. Mother had given her a key to let herself out of the house when she was finished vacuuming and washing the floors, and she was always gone when we got home for lunch. She seemed to be able to find things in the stores that nobody else could and was always offering to get mother tea and other items that were rationed. Mother refused because she said the foods must have been stolen.

I had heard Mother talking to neighbours about the Black Market. I had never seen a black market and I wondered if it was like the blackout. Blackout was what people called the turning off of all the streetlights, the covered windows, and the unlit trains and train stations. Whatever the black market was, I knew it was a bad thing, and people who sold things there could be sent to jail. I could not imagine Mrs Smithers doing anything illegal.

My eighth birthday was on the first of March and mother wanted to make me a cake. She looked in the larder and found that she had very little sugar left. She was surprised because she had cut down the amount of sugar she put in her tea to almost nothing. When Mrs Smithers came for her pay, she once again asked mother if she needed any sugar. Mother decided that for my sake she would ignore her conscience this once and said, "Yes, I do."

Mrs Smithers grinned and said, "I've got some at 'ome. I'll get it right away." She was back again very quickly and handed mother a small bag of sugar. "'Ere yer go luv. That'll be sixpence."

"Thank you, Mrs Smithers. I shan't be needing anything more."

"Yer know where I am if yer do." She tapped a finger on the side of her nose. "I've got me contacts."

Mother smiled and quickly shut the door.

I invited Vicky and Violet to tea on my birthday. We had jam sandwiches and the cake was delicious. Mother sent two slices across the road for Mr and Mrs Davis. As we waved Vicky and Violet goodbye, mother looked at me. "If Mr or Mrs Davis asks where I got the sugar for your cake, don't tell them, Katie. It might get Mrs Smithers into trouble."

I promised I would not. It might get mother into trouble too.

In March, jam was put on the list of rationed foods.

"At least we won't go short yet," said Mother taking a new jar of jam from the neat row sitting in the larder. This was on Monday. By teatime on Friday, I was scraping the bottom of the jar to put on my bread. Mother went to the larder to get another jar.

She came back looking puzzled. "That's funny." With a pop, she prised the lid off the new jar. "I was sure there were ten jars left on Monday. There's only eight now. Have you opened another one, Katie?"

"No, Mummy. I can't unscrew the new jars."

"No, of course you can't. Anyway, I would have washed up the empty jar and I don't remember doing so. Oh well. I must have miscounted."

The following Wednesday when Vicky and I came home from school, I heard voices coming from my house, so instead of going with Vicky, I went home. As I reached the back door, it was suddenly flung open. Mrs Smithers pushed past me and scuttled down the path to the road.

Mother came behind her shouting, "And don't bother coming back!"

She saw me standing there and stood back. "Sorry Katie. Come in."

She followed me into the kitchen.

"What's happened?" I asked.

Mother sat at the kitchen table and sighed. "I came home early and found Mrs Smithers spooning sugar from our little bag of sugar into one of her own. When I asked her what she was doing, she tried to tell me some tale about our bag leaking. I looked at it. There was no hole or slit in it and when I told her I thought she was stealing the sugar, she pretended to cry. Made a lot of noise but there were no tears. In the end, she admitted that she has been taking sugar since it became rationed."

Mother started checking the contents of the larder and suddenly began to laugh.

"What are you laughing at?" I pleaded

"Oh, Katie. It just occurred to me, the sugar I bought from Mrs Smithers to make your cake was probably our own. I am willing to bet she took two of our jars of jam too. I wonder who is enjoying those?"

When Helen came home from work, we told her about Mrs Smithers and the sugar, and we fell about laughing again.

"What a cheek," laughed Helen. "You must admit she has gumption. Thank goodness she isn't on Hitler's side."

With Mrs Smithers gone, Mother, Helen, and I spent Sunday afternoons vacuuming and doing the laundry. "Better the day, better the deed," mother always said.

The Blitz ended in May, and the air raids lessened. Helen's warden duties were less frequent and we only went into the air raid shelter when the siren went. This sometimes meant that Mother woke me from my sleep in the middle of the night. Half asleep, I would follow her down the garden to stumble into the air raid shelter and fall onto the hastily made-up bunk bed.

I was still missing Lucy, Ollie, and Trot. Sometimes, when mother put my food in front of me, I saw something that Ollie would like and I pushed it aside to give to him. Then I would remember and have to fight back the tears. I knew that Mother missed Lucy and Ollie too, and that she was also sad for Father. I decided to suggest that we get a kitten.

"Oh I don't think so, Katie. I don't think a cat would eat veggies like Ollie did, and we don't get much meat for three people."

"But Mummy, I am so lonely."

"I know Katie. I'm lonely too. Perhaps you should write to Daddy and ask what he thinks. Sit down and write to him while I'm getting the tea. I'll post the letter tomorrow."

I sighed but knew that I would have to ask my father. I went to the writing desk and found a small sheet of paper and a pencil. I began to write:

DEAR DADDY,

I AM SORRY THAT OLLIE DIED. YOU MUST BE VERY SAD. MUMMY AND I MADE A LOVLY GRAVE UNDER THE ROSE BUSH AND MUMMY MADE A CROSS FROM TWO TWIGS. YOU CAN SEE IT WHEN YOU COME HOME. LUCY, TROT AND THE FISH ARE WITH HIM NOW. I AM VERY LONLY WITHOUT THEM. I THINK I WOULD LIKE TO HAVE A KITTEN BUT MUMMY SAYS I SHOUD ASK YOU FIRST.

COULD I, PLEASE? I COULD CALL HER LUCY TWO IF ITS A GIRL KITTEN AND LUKE IF ITS A BOY.

I HOPE YOU ARE SAFE. MUMMY AND I PRAY TO GOD AND JESUS FOR YOU EVERY NIGHT.

I MISS YOU. WRITE SOON.

LOVE,

KATIE XXXXXX

I folded the letter and put it on the table beside mother's plate.

Mother picked it up. "I'll write a letter and put them both in the same envelope," she said.

The next morning, I made sure that Mother had taken the letters with her when she went to work. That night when I said my bedtime prayer, I added a new request. "Please God, let me have a kitten."

I knew it might take a long time for the letter to reach father on his ship, but when two weeks had passed, I began watching for the postman every morning. When he did turn into our gate, I ran to the door to wait for the letter to come through the letterbox. It was always something official looking. "Bills," mother said.

It was four weeks before a letter came with my father's handwriting on the envelope.

"Mummy," I cried excitedly. "Daddy's letter has come." I ran into the kitchen and thrust the precious envelope into mother's hand. She opened it and pulled out two sheets of paper. One she kept and the other she handed to me.

"There you go Katie. Here's your letter."

I unfolded the piece of paper and read:

MAY, 1941

MY DEAR KATIE,

I HOPE YOU ARE GETTING TO SLEEP EARLIER THAN YOU WERE WHEN I WAS AT HOME. IF YOU DON'T GET ENOUGH SLEEP YOU WILL GET SICK.

YES, I AM VERY SAD ABOUT OLLIE AND ALL OUR PETS. YOU ASK ABOUT GETTING A KITTEN. A KITTEN WOULD BE A BIG RESPONSIBILITY. I THINK YOU SHOULD ASK MUMMY.

GOODNIGHT AND GOD BLESS.

LOTS OF LOVE.

DADDY. XXXXX

I felt my heart drop. A tear fell onto the paper.

Mother finished reading her letter and looked up. "What did Daddy have to say?" she asked brightly.

"Nothing much."

"Katie, what's wrong? Did Daddy say you can't have a kitten?"

"Not 'xactly. He said a kitten was a big responsibility. What's he mean?"

"Well Daddy is right. He means that we might not be able to feed a kitten properly right now."

I sighed. "I s'pose".

"Never mind, sweetie. When the war ends and Daddy comes home, we can have a kitten and a puppy. How about that?"

I smiled and put my arms around mother's neck. I kissed her cheek.

"P'raps we can have a rabbit too," I ventured.

Mother laughed. "Perhaps. Now it's time for school."

I ran to the Davis' house and banged the knocker. The door opened and Vicky rushed out. Violet stood in the doorway. I told them about getting a puppy and a kitten and *maybe* a rabbit when the war ended.

"Can I stroke the kitten?" Violet asked.

"Course you can," I said happily. "And we'll all take the puppy to play in the park.

Chapter 8

May saw the start of another round of rationing. Cheese was added to the list and in June, eggs. Also in June, a new ration book was created for clothes. Everyone was given a clothing book with coloured coupons in it. Every item of clothing was given a point value in coupons and the shopkeepers cut out the appropriate coupon. When the clothing book was first issued, every adult was given an allocation of sixty-six points to last one year. In 1943, this was reduced to forty points and rose to forty-eight points in 1944. In July, coal was rationed, not because there was a lack of coal in the ground, but because many of the miners had been called up to serve in the forces. Fresh eggs had been hard to get before, but now we could only have one fresh egg a week. Even the powdered eggs were cut to one, twelve-egg packet of egg powder a month. In August, mother began making jam again. At least we would not be eating bread and bread sandwiches in the winter.

One morning in late August, my Aunt Em called on us. She looked unhappy and talked quietly to mother for a few minutes. I heard mother say, "Don't worry. I am sure it will be for the best." Mother saw me listening and said, "Aunty Em has some good news. Jenny is getting married."

I was delighted. My cousin Jenny was seventeen and I loved her. She had no brothers or sisters so I said we could pretend she was my sister. Jenny's father had died before I was born, and Aunt Em had to go to work. When she was still going to school, Jenny often called at our house on her way home. I think she did not like going home to an empty house. We spent many hours dressing my dolls and on rainy days, Jenny read to me. She had left school in July 1940 and gone to work. I had seen less of her since then. I knew that she had a boyfriend but had not met him. She confided to me that she had fallen in love, "like the ladies in the films, do."

Jenny's boyfriend was nineteen years old and an airman in the RAF. When I met him, I thought he was very handsome, like a prince in a fairy tale. His name belonged in a fairy tale too. It was Arthur, Arthur Merriweather. I could imagine him as Prince Arthur, pulling the magic sword from the stone, and holding it in triumph above his head. After Aunt Em left, I asked my mother, "Why is Aunty Em not happy about Jenny getting married?"

Mother shrugged. "I think she would prefer Jenny to wait until she is older."

The day of the Registry Office wedding in late September, was sunny and warm. I was the only bridesmaid, dressed in my Sunday dress, and carrying a small posy of flowers. Jenny looked lovely and Arthur was handsome in his blue airman's uniform. I hoped that when I got married, I would marry an airman like Arthur.

The next day he returned to his aerodrome.

A couple of weeks later, Aunt Em and Jenny came to visit. Jenny was obviously bursting to tell us something, but Aunt insisted that we all sit down before anything was said.

Mother put the kettle on the fire to boil water for tea and sat down. "Well what brings you here today?" she asked.

Jenny grinned and patted her stomach. "I'm going to have a baby," she almost shrieked with excitement.

I rushed over to her and hugged her. "That's lovely!" I shouted.

"When?" Mother asked.

Before Jenny could speak, Aunt said, "Sometime in the spring."

Aunt's and mother's eyes met and they both nodded.

I was delighted. I had always hoped that I would have a baby brother or sister and Jenny having a baby was the next best thing. "Can I help you look after the baby, Jenny?"

"Course you can. I shall need a lot of help," she said. She stood up and we danced around the room to celebrate.

I saw mother go over to aunt Em. She patted her on the shoulder and said something to her. Then she made the tea and set out cups and a small plate of biscuits.

"Come on you two. Sit down. You're making me dizzy and Lord knows what you're doing to the baby," said aunt, crossly I thought.

We sat down but I could not take my eyes off Jenny. She looked so lovely and happy. I could not wait for 'sometime in the Spring,' to come.

The first week of November brought the usual fog. School was let out early on two days because of it.

On November fifth, Mrs Deane read the story of Guy Fawkes to us. We all knew the story of the time in 1605 when a group of English Catholics plotted to kill King James I and restore Catholicism as the religion of the United Kingdom. They intended to blow up the House of Lords during the State Opening of Parliament on the fifth of November.

The barrels of gunpowder had been hidden in a cellar beneath the House of Lords. Guy Fawkes or Guido Fawkes, a member of the group, was assigned to guard the gunpowder on the night before it was to be lit. Unfortunately for him, the plot was revealed and he was arrested around midnight on November fourth and was executed on November fifth. The king proclaimed that every year on November fifth, the English people should celebrate his salvation by burning Guy Fawkes in effigy. Every year since then, the English had done just that, in later years adding fireworks to the celebration...until the outbreak of the Second World War, that is. The blackout put an end to bonfires and fireworks until the war came to an end.

As Mrs Deane read, I thought back to the time before the air raids when Dougie, Jimmy, and I with help from our fathers, made a stuffed effigy of Guy Fawkes; a Guy. We put the almost life-sized Guy on a cart and stood at the corner of the street. We took the hat from the Guy's head and placed it on the ground, calling to passers-by;

"Remember, remember,
The fifth of November
Gunpowder, treason, and plot.
I see no reason
Why gunpowder treason
Should ever be forgot.
So please put a penny in the old Guy's hat"

With the pennies we were given, we went to the newspaper shop and bought fireworks. The first week in November, my father and Mr King built a large bonfire in our garden, with twigs from pruning and other garden refuse. They bought boxes of fireworks to add to the sparklers and bangers that we had bought.

On the night of November fifth, houses where there were children had bonfires in the gardens. Father put our Guy on top of the bonfire and used matches to set the bonfire alight. My mother scrubbed large potatoes that father had grown and put them at the bottom of the fire to cook. Father and Mr King lit the rockets and Katherine-wheels, while Dougie, Jimmy, and I ran around the garden waving sparklers in the air. The night sky filled with the sounds of the rockets screaming through the air and explosions that sent many-coloured streams of light falling to earth. Oohs and aahs, bangs and shrieks came from almost every garden the length of the street.

By bedtime, the fires had burned down, the potatoes were cooked, and the air was filled with smoke. Mother pulled the now-cooked potatoes from the fire, split them in half, and put a knob of butter into each half. We held them in our gloved hands and ate them, the butter dribbling down our chins. We washed the potatoes down with mugs of steaming cocoa.

Sitting in the classroom, I could remember the taste of the potato oozing butter, and feel the heat from the cup of cocoa in my cold hands. The next morning was always foggy and the smell of burning hung on the damp air.

On the night of November the fifth, 1938, we did not know that it would be seven years before we celebrated Guy Fawkes Night again. This November fifth, the lights in the sky could be from searchlights and tracer bullets; the shrieks and bangs from bombs falling through the air.

The following Wednesday afternoon, I galloped home pretending I was riding a pony. I trotted into the garden and dismounted. As I opened the back door, I heard my grandfather's voice coming from the kitchen. "You'll only have to look after her for a few weeks," I heard him say.

My ears pricked up. Who could be coming to visit? Perhaps a little girl whose home had been bombed. I ran into the kitchen and threw myself onto grandfather's knee. "Who are we going to look after?" I asked.

Grandfather made a face as he put down his cup of weak, sugarless, wartime tea into its saucer. I knew he did not enjoy tea much when it did not have three spoonfuls of sugar in it. He kissed the top of my head.

"Not a 'who,' Katie, an 'it.' I'm too old to keep chickens now, and I want to get rid of the chicken houses to make room for vegetables. My last hen has gone broody and I thought your Mummy might like to fatten her up for Christmas. Then on Christmas Day, I can come here and have chicken for my Christmas dinner."

"Oh yes," I cried. With all food rationed, Christmas dinner would probably be sausages. I liked sausages but it would be nice to have chicken for a change. Mother hated wartime sausages. They had so much bread and fat in them that no matter how many times she pricked them with a fork, they burst in the frying pan and splashed her with hot fat.

"Where would I put it?" Mother asked.

"You can keep it in the greenhouse. There's nothing growing in there at this time of year. I'll come round on Christmas Eve and kill it for you."

Mother still looked doubtful. "What do I feed it, to fatten it up?"

"I'll bring you a bag of meal and you can add boiled potato peelings to it to make a mash," said Grandfather.

We ate lots of potatoes because mother grew them in the garden. There would be plenty of peelings for the chicken.

Grandfather lifted me off his knee and stood up. "That's settled then," he said decisively. "Thanks for the tea. I'll be round in the morning with the chicken."

"Thanks Dad," said mother as she closed the door behind him. She looked worried.

I was excited. "Don't worry, Mummy. I'll help you look after it." I gave her a big hug.

Mother smiled and I thought about having a chicken for Christmas dinner. I could almost smell it cooking.

"I'll hold you to that Katie, when the greenhouse needs cleaning out," she laughed, returning my hug.

When Helen came home from work I told her about the chicken.

"Ooh, chicken for Christmas dinner. Scrumptious. I can't wait, " she said.

As I ate my breakfast of toast and jam the next morning, I heard the tinkle of Grandfather's bicycle bell as he rode into the back garden. I ran out to see him lifting a sack of meal from the carrier over the back wheel. Another sack hung from the handlebars. It was jiggling about and making squawking noises. Grandfather lifted a backpack from his shoulders and took from it a water bottle. He handed it to Mother, who had come to join us. "Fill this with water please," he said. Then he pulled out a small dish and a bag of tiny stones that he emptied into the dish.

"This is grit," he explained. "A chicken has no teeth and it needs this to help it chew up its food."

He opened the sack and took out a metal cup with some meal in it. "You carry this," he said handing it to me.

Mother returned with the water bottle and Grandfather took the wriggling sack from the bicycle handlebars. "Right! Let's show this old hen its new home."

I followed Grandfather and Mother followed me, down the path to the greenhouse. Grandfather laid the sack down while he opened the greenhouse door. He put the dish of grit on the floor, took the cup, and scattered the meal onto the dirt. Then he took the water bottle from Mother and placed that next to the pot of grit.

I squatted beside him as he knelt down and untied the string around the top of the sack. After a little struggle, a sorry-looking brown hen stumbled out, and began scratching in the dirt.

"I fed it before I came," said Grandfather. "Feed it a cup of meal and potato peelings tonight, and then night and morning until Christmas Eve."

While Mother and Grandfather walked back to the house, I peeped through the window in the greenhouse door. The chicken was scratching at the dirt and picking out the meal. I could hear her clucking to herself.

It was hard to concentrate on schoolwork that day, and several times I jumped as Mrs Deane thumped the desk with her ruler. At lunchtime, I rushed down to the greenhouse to see if the chicken was happy in her makeshift home. As I looked through the window, the chicken cocked her head on one side, and seemed to be looking right back at me. Then she went back to scratching in the dirt.

The afternoon seemed even longer than the morning had been, and I was relieved when the bell sounded to end classes for the day. I ran as hard as I could and arrived home panting and red in the face. When I erupted into the house, the smell of boiling potato peelings wrapped itself around me.

"Oh good," Mother greeted me. "You're just in time to help me feed the chicken."

She lifted the pot of peelings from the fire and drained the water into the sink. Smelly clouds of steam filled the kitchen. The smell followed us out to the garden shed where Mother added a cup of meal to the pot. The cold air created clouds of even more horrible smells as she mashed the meal into the peelings. Then she emptied the whole mess into a chipped dish.

I skipped ahead of Mother down the path to the greenhouse. When the chicken saw me looking through the window, she came over to the door to investigate. Mother peered over my shoulder, and waving the dish, she made shooing noises at the chicken. At the sight of food, the chicken became very excited, and flapping its wings, it jumped up at the door, clucking loudly.

"Katie, open the door slowly, just wide enough for me to squeeze the dish through," said Mother. "We don't want to have to chase the chicken around the garden."

I did as Mother instructed and using the dish as a battering ram, she pushed the chicken backwards into the greenhouse. As soon as the dish was on the floor, Mother slammed the door shut. The chicken happily attacked the food and Mother gave a relieved sigh. I wondered how she was going to get the dish out.

"We'll have to get up earlier in the mornings if we have to feed the chicken before I go to work and you to school, so come on Katie, let's put up the window boards and then have our tea."

I would have liked to stay and watch the chicken, but it was already getting dark and the air raid warning might go as soon as night fell. I looked in the window one more time. "Goodnight chicken. See you in the morning."

The next morning, Mother put the food in a second dish, and while she backed the chicken into the greenhouse, I slipped in and removed the dirty dish and the water bottle. I ran to the house to refill the bottle and, as I reached the back door, grandfather rode up with a bale of straw on his back.

"I've bought some straw for the chicken to make a nest in. It will keep it warm at night," he explained. "I'll put it in the shed," he said to Mother as she came up to us. "I'll show you how much to use at a time, and then you can rake it out and put in new when it is dirty."

In the shed, Grandfather cut through the twine on the straw and took off a large armful. "How is the old bird this morning?" he asked me as I hopped and skipped beside him on the way to the greenhouse.

"She seems okay, but Mummy's afraid that she will get out when we open the door to put her food in."

"The chicken won't escape. It's too dozy. Chickens have very small brains. Come on I'll show you."

At the greenhouse, Grandfather opened the door wide and stepped inside. The chicken clucked in protest and backed away from him. He put the straw down in the corner, and immediately, the chicken went over to it and began to rearrange it with her feet. She scratched at it and kicked it about until it formed a mound with a dent in the middle. Then she sat in the dent and looked round contentedly.

"It thinks it's going to raise a brood of chicks," said Grandfather. "It won't venture far from that corner."

I was still holding the empty water bottle. "Oh I forgot to fill this. I'll run back and do that."

When I returned with the water bottle, Grandfather was standing outside the closed door of the greenhouse. "There you go. Just open the door and go in. You won't disturb it," he said.

I did as I was told and the chicken just clucked quietly at me as I replaced the bottle. As I left, I said to the chicken, "Goodbye. I'm going to school now but I'll be back at lunchtime."

Grandfather frowned. "It's only a chicken, Katie. It hasn't got enough brains to understand you."

I frowned back. "I don't care. I like talking to *her*."

After a few days, I got used to the smell of boiling potato peelings. It was the first thing that greeted me every afternoon when I came home from school. In the mornings, Mother used cold peelings left over from the night before to mix with the meal. I took the food to the chicken.

"Good morning chicken. Did you sleep well?" I called out as I opened the door.

The chicken climbed from its nest of straw and fluffed its feathers. I put the dish down and the chicken clucked before picking at the food.

"I can't stop now. I have to go to school," I told her. "Have a nice day."

In the afternoons when I fed the chicken, I would stay with her and watch her eat. Sometimes, a weak beam of sunlight shone through the remaining glass panes and the chicken's feathers took on a reddish glow. I thought she was beautiful. She soon got used to me and came to greet me when I opened the greenhouse door. I loved the way she cocked her head to one side and then the other, to look up at me, and the soft clucking noises she made in greeting. When the food had been eaten, the chicken settled in its nest for the night.

On Saturdays, I cleaned out the greenhouse. I removed the straw and swept the dirt floor. I scrubbed the table that used to hold father's tomato plant seedlings and even washed those greenhouse windows that had escaped breaking when the bomb fell. When the new straw was in place and the chicken had rearranged it to its liking, I would squat on my heels and talk to her. I told her about the pets I'd had before the war and how much I missed them. I took the collection of shrapnel that I kept in a little case in my bedroom to the greenhouse and showed it to the chicken. And I talked about playing at dogfights with toy aeroplanes with Dougie and Jimmy, when they lived next door.

One Saturday morning when I was talking to the chicken, grandfather appeared in the doorway of the greenhouse.

"How are things going, Katie?" he asked.

"Oh Grandpa, I think the chicken likes me."

"I think a chicken likes anyone who feeds it. Is it eating well?"

"Yes, and I clean the straw out every week so she'll be comfy. I think she is very pretty. What kind of chicken is she, Grandpa?""

"She's a Rhode Island Red."

"Oh, that's why her feathers look a bit reddish when the sun shines on them."

"Yes, I suppose so. I've never given it much thought."

"I am going to give her a name. What do you think is a good name for a chicken, Grandpa?"

Grandfather shook his head. "I shouldn't do that Katie. The chicken won't recognize a name. It's not like a dog that comes when you call."

I scowled and folded my arms across my chest.

Grandfather ruffled my hair. "Don't be cross, Katie. A chicken is useful but it's not a pet. I'd better go and say hello to your mother. I'll see you on Christmas Eve."

I turned back to the chicken. It was scratching in the dirt. "I don't care what Grandpa says. I am going to give you a name. Would you like a name?"

The chicken stopped scratching. Its head turned from side to side as it looked up at me.

I squatted in the dirt and studied her. "What shall I call you? Maizy? Chicky?"

The chicken clucked softly.

"That's it!" I cried. "I shall call you Clucky. Do you like that name?"

The chicken clucked again and waggled its head.

"Yes you do like it. I shan't tell anyone I have given you a name because they'll only say I'm silly, but you know and I know that you like your name."

From that day, I always thought of the chicken as Clucky and I spent every moment I could talking to her. Clucky listened when I told her that I was worried about something at school, and I told her when a letter came from Father. When there had been an air raid at night, my first thought in the morning was of Clucky. Before going to the house, I visited the greenhouse to make sure she was safe. Some of the glass in the greenhouse got cracked by bomb blast, and I put tape on all the windows so that they would not shatter during a raid and fall on her. No matter what Clucky was doing, when she saw me looking through the door window, she came over to greet me. She never flew up at the door when I brought her food, but moved out of the way so I could get in.

Chapter 9

Helen was working in a government office in central London, and I saw little of her. She left the house before I got up in the morning, and most evenings I was in bed when she returned.

One day in late November, a brown envelope addressed to her came in the morning post. Mother frowned when she saw it. That evening, I was still up when Helen got home. Mother showed Helen the envelope and said, "I think it might be bad news."

Helen tore the envelope open and read the contents. Now she was frowning.

"Yes, you're right, Mum. I have to report to the recruiting office next Monday."

Mother burst into tears and I ran and put my arms around Helen's neck. What would I do without my sister? She was the person I looked up to. She was kind and clever and pretty. I wanted to be like her when I grew up. She unpicked her old woollen cardigans and knit the wool into small sweaters for me. I had almost grown out of my favourite one, and if Helen went away there wouldn't be another one. She was a girl. What would she do in a war?

When she reported to the recruiting office, she was told to report to an army camp on her birthday. That was a week away.

The day before Helen was to leave, mother made a small cake, for her birthday. We sang "Happy Birthday" to her and mother added, "And come home safely," instead of, "And many more."

The next morning, mother and I went to the train station with Helen to see her off on her journey to the camp, to start her new life as a soldier. She looked very smart in her khaki jacket and forage cap, set at a jaunty angle on her newly cropped hair. There were tears as the train drew away from the platform. Other parents were waving goodbye to children or husbands. Soon, the only people in our town would be old or ill men and women, mothers with children, and a few people in factories and civilian jobs important to the war effort. When the train disappeared from view, we quietly walked out of the station and trudged slowly home.

One afternoon, two weeks before Christmas, the 'shoe lady' visited the school. Because children kept growing, a lady came to the school twice a year and measured our feet. I knew that if my feet had grown, I would be given a coupon to take to the shoe shop to buy another pair of shoes. The last time my feet were measured, the lady said I did not need new shoes, because there was still room to grow in the ones I was wearing. I sat at my desk, wiggling my toes to feel if they were too close to the toe of my shoe. I hoped my feet had grown because then I could have new shoes for Christmas.

Miss Wilkins, my Fourth Year teacher, called my name and I hurried to the front of the class, where the lady looked up my record in her file. On the floor was a long piece of wood like a ruler, with a place to put one's heel at one end and a sliding arm at the other end. I took off my shoe and stood on the ruler, my heel loosely touching the end. I stretched out my big toe and the lady moved the arm up to it. She marked her file.

"Your foot has grown half an inch since you had your last pair of shoes, young lady. Here you are." She handed me a coupon. "Give this to your mother. Tell her to get a shoe for you that will allow for future growth."

I held the coupon as though it were a pound note. I felt like jumping for joy. Instead I said, "Thank you, Miss. I'll tell her."

When school ended for the day, I ran all the way home; the coupon still clasped in my hand.

After I had given mother the coupon and told her about getting shoes that "allow for growth," I ran down to the greenhouse to give Clucky the good news. Clucky was sitting on her straw, but when she saw me she got up. She cocked her head as though listening as I told her about having my foot measured, and showed her how I had stretched my toe out as far as I could.

"Mummy says, as it is Saturday tomorrow, we can go out after lunch and see if the shop has any shoes that fit me. But I won't wear them until Christmas."

The chicken clucked once and turned back to its nest.

"Oh, I'm sorry Clucky," I said, as I realised that at Christmas, Clucky would not be able to see my shoes. "I'll put them on tomorrow just to show to you," I added sadly.

The next day, Mother and I went to the High Street to look for shoes. There were three shoe shops still open, but the first two had no shoes left in my size. I was getting tired and upset. I had hoped to be able to get a pair of shoes with a strap and buckle instead of the black lace-ups I had been wearing for the last year, but now it seemed I would be lucky to find anything.

"Never mind," said Mother. "There's still the shop at the Broadway. I expect everyone who was given a coupon went to the shops we've been to because they're the nearest. It won't take long to walk to the end of the High Street."

It didn't take long but to me it seemed we walked to the end of the world. There was no one else in the shop when we opened the door. A bell above the door rang and immediately a small lady with grey hair, drawn back in a bun, came through a door at the back of the shop.

"Good afternoon, ma'am, miss. What can I do for you?"

"My daughter needs new shoes," said Mother, guiding me to a seat and sitting down beside me.

The sales lady pulled a stool in front of me. She sat on the stool and put a measuring block, like the one the 'shoe lady' at school used, on the floor between us.

"Take off your shoes and stand on this, and we'll see what size shoe you need."

I did as I was told and the lady measured my right foot. "Now the other one, please. Good. I'm sure I can find something for you," she said smiling at me.

After a few minutes the sales lady returned with two boxes. I suddenly felt much better. The lady opened one of them. "Now this pair is the same as the ones you have now," she said brightly and produced a pair of black lace-ups.

My heart sank.

The lady looked at me and raised her eyebrows. "Were you hoping to change the style?"

I felt myself blushing.

Mother leaned round to look at me. She spoke to the lady. "Do you have another style?"

"Oh yes!" She leaned down and opened the second box. "This is not so heavy looking but is quite serviceable. Do you want to try this one on?"

I looked at the shoe the sales lady was holding. It was shiny black with a single strap across the foot and a silver buckle at the side. I closed my eyes and said a silent prayer. "Please God, let it fit."

"Give me your right foot please."

I put my foot into the lady's hand and felt the shoe slip onto it. The lady fastened the buckle and put my foot onto the floor. "There. How does that feel?"

I did not care how it felt. If it pinched my toes horribly, I would have said it was fine.

The lady was pinching the top of the shoe to find where my toes were. "Yes, that seems to fit, with a little room for growth. Let's try the other foot."

I sat again while the lady put the left shoe on me.

"Now walk around a bit to make sure the shoes are not going to rub anywhere. There's a mirror over there you can look in."

I walked up and down the shop three times, stopping each time to admire my feet in the mirror. Mother was talking to the sales lady and showing her the coupon.

I heard the lady saying, "I am sure they will last until she grows out of them. It's so hard for little girls to have to wear the same shoes every day. They ought to be able to like what they are wearing."

I watched as Mother gave the sales lady some coins and the bell on the till rang as the drawer opened to take in the money.

The sales lady came around the counter with a paper bag. "Shall I put the shoes in here or are you going to wear them home?"

I looked at my feet and then at the old black lace-ups left by the chair. I sighed and bent to take the new shoes off.

"Yes, please put them in the bag. I'm going to save them for Christmas Day."

"Very wise," said the sales lady taking the shoes. "You will look very pretty I'm sure."

When we came out of the shop it was dark and cloudy, and we could see no stars or the moon. We took out our torches and began the walk home. I was so pleased with my new shoes that the way home seemed much shorter than the way out had been. We were soon unlocking the door to the house.

"We shall have to put the blackout boards up in the dark tonight, Katie," said mother as she closed the door. We made our way into the front room and using our torches managed to find the boards and put them in place. Mother turned on the light and she and I gasped. Sleeping in the armchair by the fire was Father!

The light roused him and he woke, shaking himself. I rushed at him and flung my arms around his neck.

"Careful there, Katie. You'll strangle me."

Mother now joined me and for a few minutes the room was filled with laughter and crying and questions and answers.

"How long have you been here?"

"About an hour. I've been travelling since yesterday. There was snow on the line and the train couldn't move for hours."

"Are you going to stay with us now, Daddy?

"No, I'm sorry, Katie. I have to go back again tomorrow."

"Are you hungry? I'll make something to eat." Mother went into the kitchen and I heard water running into the kettle and cupboard doors being opened and shut. I remembered my shoes. I took them out of the bag and gave them to Father.

"My feet have grown so much that I had to get new shoes," I told him proudly. "I'm not going to wear them till Christmas. Will you be here for Christmas, Daddy?"

"No. But I'll be thinking of you."

Mother came in carrying a tray with cups and saucers, a steaming teapot, sugar, milk, a pot of jam, and slices of bread. "Here, Katie. Toast this bread on the fire, please."

I put a slice of bread on the toasting fork that stood beside the fire and began toasting.

After I toasted the slices of bread, father spread them with Mummy's homemade jam, and soon we were sitting down to tea and toast by the warm fire. Afterwards, he helped Mummy wash and dry the dishes and I put them away. Then we sat by the fire and found pictures in the flames. Father made up stories of princesses and princes and wicked witches who put spells on them and good fairies who put everything right again.

"Have you written to Father Christmas yet?" he asked.

I knew Father Christmas did not really exist, but I did not want to tell Mother and Father and spoil things for them so I said, "No."

"Well get a piece of paper and write to him now."

I hurried to the desk and found a small sheet of paper and a pencil. What could I ask for? I chewed the end of the pencil, thinking. There would not be an orange in my stocking, but there were books in a second-hand bookstore in the High Street. I printed, "I would like a book please, Santa. Love Katie," and handed it to Father.

He looked before folding it into four. "Mail the letter up the chimney," he said, handing it back to me. "There's a good breeze blowing so it will soon reach the North Pole."

I carefully held it over the dying fire beneath the chimney and it rose with the curling smoke, up to the night sky.

I was falling asleep on Father's lap before Mother said it was time for me to go to bed. "We won't go down to the shelter tonight," she said. "This is the only night Daddy will be home and it would be a shame to not spend it in our own beds. Come along, Katie. We'll all go up together."

Father picked me up and carried me up the stairs to my bedroom. Mother helped me to get into my pyjamas. Father tucked me into bed. "Goodnight, sweetie. I have to go very early in the morning, so I'll say goodbye now. Sleep tight and don't let the bedbugs bite."

"Goodnight, Daddy. God Bless."

When I woke in the morning, Father had gone.

Chapter 10

As Christmas drew nearer, it became harder and harder for me to think of Clucky as Christmas dinner. I tried to get mother to feel the same way.

"Isn't she good, Mummy? Look at how shiny her feathers are and she really doesn't make much mess, does she?"

"You know, Mummy, I really like sausages don't you?"

"It takes a lot of work to cook a chicken, doesn't it Mummy?"

"Won't you miss the chicken when she's gone?"

But Mother said she would not miss the chicken, and she was looking forward to a nice chicken dinner on Christmas Day.

The night before Christmas Eve, I took Clucky her supper. I closed the greenhouse door and sat down on the dirt floor. I put the dish of food down in front of Clucky. While she was eating, I talked to her.

"I am very sorry, Clucky. This is the last time I shall see you, so I am going to say goodbye now. I've loved having you to talk to and look after. Tomorrow, Grandpa is coming to..."

I could not put into words what Grandfather was going to do. "You see, Mummy is really happy that she is going to have a nice Christmas dinner and she hates sausages. No one understands that you're not like other chickens. Grandpa says that chickens are stupid birds and don't understand anything. But I know that you understand me. I must go now. Mummy will wonder what I'm doing. Goodbye Clucky. I love you and I'll always remember you."

I stroked Clucky's head and quickly left the greenhouse. I closed the door without looking back and ran into the house.

The next morning, I sat staring at the bread on my plate. I had cried myself to sleep the night before, and now I felt too miserable to cry. I knew that in a few hours, Clucky would be dead. There was no way that I could eat my breakfast and I knew that I would not be able to eat my Christmas dinner either.

Mother was preparing Clucky's food and I breathed in the funny smell of meal and potato peelings for the last time. I closed my eyes, and in my head I saw Clucky waiting eagerly at the greenhouse door for her breakfast.

"Are you going to take this to the chicken, Katie? It's the last time you'll be able to."

I looked down at my plate so that mother would not see how close I was to crying. "No not today, Mummy."

Mother shrugged and went out of the kitchen.

I felt salty tears trickle down my cheeks.

I was trying to dry my tears when I heard mother running back to the house. She fell into the kitchen, apron flapping, and eyes wide with astonishment. She flopped onto a chair. "We can't kill the chicken," she gasped.

I couldn't believe my ears. "What?" I asked.

"We can't kill the chicken," she repeated.

"Why?" I cried with delight.

"Because…" Mother stopped to regain her breath. "Because she has laid an egg!"

Mother held out her hand and there on the palm, was a perfect, brown-shelled egg. I could hardly believe my eyes. I hugged mother and without even waiting to put on a coat, I rushed out of the house and down the garden to the greenhouse.

Clucky was contentedly picking at the food in her dish, unaware that she had saved her own life. She clucked loudly and struggled when I knelt down and tried to hug her.

"Oh Clucky, I am so happy. We'll have to have exploding sausages for Christmas dinner after all."

Grandfather arrived after lunch and was a little upset that mother would not let him kill the chicken.

"But Grandpa," I explained, "the chicken is a mother now."

"Yes, and if she keeps on laying, we'll have eggs to eat," said Mother.

"I shouldn't hold your breath," said Grandfather. "She'll soon go broody again."

I was much too happy to worry about the future. When I took Clucky her breakfast on Christmas morning, I found another egg in the nest of straw and Mother and I ate boiled eggs for breakfast that morning.

Grandpa was a bit put out to not have chicken for Christmas dinner, but Mother agreed with me that the sausages we had for dinner were the best we had ever tasted.

To add insult to injury, in the New Year, we heard from both Father and Helen that they had been served turkey on Christmas Day.

Boxing Day morning, I ran down to the greenhouse with Clucky's breakfast. I found her sitting on the nest making a noise I had not heard before. To my ear, Clucky sounded pleased with herself. After a few minutes, she stood up and ruffling her feathers, went to her food dish. I looked in the straw and there was another egg.

"Oh, you clever thing," I cried. "Now you have to do this every day, and then Grandpa won't be able to kill you."

But I knew that grandfather was probably right, and that when Clucky stopped laying eggs he would want to kill her. It was very worrying.

December 1941 brought disasters for Britain in the Far East. Having marched into China, the Japanese turned its armies toward Burma. They declared war on Britain and on December eleventh, Japanese aircraft attacked airfields south of Rangoon. The battle for

Rangoon did not end until March 7th, 1942. December was also bad for the United States of America, although the disaster only affected them and proved beneficial to Britain and mainland Europe. On December seventh, Japan attacked the United States Navy at Pearl Harbour. A treaty that had previously been signed by Japan, Germany, and Italy automatically made those three countries at war with the United States, and the United States at war with them. Churchill had been trying unsuccessfully to persuade President Roosevelt to join the Allies, and now he got his wish.

The British forces were also engaged in a battle with Japan over Hong Kong. The Battle for Hong Kong began on December 8th, 1941 and ended on Christmas Day. The Crown Colony of Hong Kong surrendered to the Empire of Japan. At the time, I was unaware of these events, and they did not cause a change in my daily life. It was not until the war ended completely that I became aware of the crimes against humanity that had been committed in Japan and Germany.

Chapter 11

1942 BABIES

The year began with rice and dried fruit added to the list of rationed food. They were joined in February by soap, so that the oils and fats used to make the soap could be saved for food. Tinned tomatoes and peas were the next casualties. By the seventeenth of March, gas and electricity had joined coal in the rationed category.

As Grandfather had predicted, Clucky did go broody again. But before that happened, I had persuaded him to build a proper hen-house and run for the chicken to live in. I painted it with some white paint I found in father's shed and I faithfully cleaned it out every week. I hoped that Grandfather would not find out that Clucky was not laying eggs. Even mother seemed to like Clucky now, and did not grumble too much about the smell of the potato peelings cooking. But the day came when Grandfather paid a visit and was told that Clucky was no longer laying.

Mother, Grandfather, and I went down to the henhouse. Grandfather looked at Clucky sitting on her nest. I stood beside him, waiting nervously for his decision. Grandfather scratched his chin and sighed a long sigh. He looked down at me. "Well, what are we going to do with this stupid bird, eh Katie?"

"Well..." I said, trying to think of a good answer.

"We could wait until she starts laying again, couldn't we?" Mother asked.

"That's an awful waste of good food. She's just too old to be a good layer, and if you don't eat her now, she'll be mighty tough by the time you do get around to it."

Now it was Mother's turn to sigh. Grandfather was scratching his chin again. Everyone was staring at Clucky.

I could stand the silence no longer. "Why does she stop laying eggs, Grandpa?"

"Because she thinks she wants to raise some chicks and she can't, because the eggs she lays won't hatch."

"Why not?"

Grandfather looked at mother. "You can answer that one," he said.

"Katie, for an egg to hatch, it has to be fertilized...I mean it has to have a Daddy. And this chicken isn't married."

I giggled. "Chickens don't get married, Mummy. You are silly."

"Yes, I know, Katie. I'll try again. You know that you have a mummy and a daddy. Mummy is a female, like you. Daddy is a male, like Grandpa. Females have eggs inside them. Males have seeds. When a seed joins an egg, a baby begins to grow. Chickens are the same. A hen makes eggs and a cockerel makes seeds. The two together make a chick. We don't have a cockerel. And," she continued quickly, seeing that I was about to ask a question. "No, we can't get a cockerel. The neighbours would complain if a cockerel crowing at sunrise woke them every morning."

It was time for me to sigh. Then a thought came into my head. Grandpa didn't have a cockerel, but he kept on getting more chickens to replace the ones he had.

"Grandpa, where did your new chickens come from?" I asked.

Grandfather stopped scratching his chin and shook his head. "Your mother may be sorry you asked that, young lady. There is one thing we could do. We could give her some chicks."

"Oh, Grandpa, could we?"

Grandfather said that we could put some china eggs under Clucky. He explained to me what we would do.

"I told you chickens weren't too bright," he said. I scowled but Grandfather ignored me and went on. "She will think they are real eggs and try to hatch them out. Then we will take away the china eggs and replace them with day-old chicks."

"Oh, yes please, Grandpa!" I cried, jumping up and down with joy.

Later that afternoon, grandfather came round with six china eggs and slipped them under Clucky, who immediately moved them around until she was sitting comfortably. She picked at the straw, pulling it around her body then settled back clucking. I would have stayed watching her until bedtime, if Grandfather had not said that the chicken would be happier if she were left in peace.

For the next few days, Clucky sat on her eggs almost all the time, leaving them only to peck at her food when I gave it to her. After a week, grandfather arrived just as mother and I were putting away the supper dishes. He was carrying a box with holes in the lid. I could hear cheeping and scuffling noises coming from it.

"Here's the chicks," grandfather announced. He lifted the lid and I saw twelve balls of chirping yellow fluff.

"Oh! They're beautiful," I said.

Mother looked over my shoulder. "Yes, I must admit they are cute."

Grandfather closed the lid. "We'll put them under the hen as soon as it gets dark. In the meantime, I'll have a cup of tea if there's one going."

While Grandfather drank his tea, mother and I put the blackout boards on the windows. I kept peeping out of the back door, so that I could tell Grandfather as soon as it was dark. After about twenty minutes I called, "Grandpa is it dark enough now?"

Grandfather looked out. "Yes I think so. The chicken should be sleeping. Now Katie, if you are coming with me, you must be quiet. We have to replace the eggs with the chicks, without upsetting the hen. She will hear the chicks and feel them but she will just think that the eggs have hatched."

I promised I would be quiet as a mouse and followed mother and grandfather, carrying the box of chicks, down the garden.

Grandfather quietly opened the door of the henhouse and put his finger to his lips to remind me that I had to be quiet. Very carefully, one at a time, he removed the china eggs from beneath the chicken, handing them to me as he did so. Every time he removed an egg, he replaced it with two chicks. Clucky wriggled and rearranged herself to make space for the chicks as Grandfather put them into the nest. When they were all safely under the hen, he closed the door and beckoned me and mother back to the house.

Back in the kitchen, he gave instructions for feeding the new arrivals. "They can eat the same as the old hen but you'll have to make up more than you have been doing. Baby chicks are pretty independent. They only need a mother for warmth really, and they grow quickly. They'll soon be fully-grown, and then you'll have to do more cleaning. They're mucky creatures."

Mother looked at me. "That's her job, Dad," she said laughing. "I'm the chicken's cook and bottle washer."

I grinned at Mother and Grandfather. "I don't mind," I said. "Thank you for bringing the chicks, Grandpa."

"My pleasure, young lady. Just don't get too fond of them. They are all females so they will all start laying eggs when they grow up. You might be able to sell some to help with the cost of their food and straw. Now I must get home before the air raid warnings start going off."

The first thing I did when I woke the next morning was to run to the henhouse. Clucky and her little family were already out in the run, busily pecking at the dirt for bits of leftover food. Clucky was talking to them and being busy. I poked my finger through the wire and stroked her feathers.

"You have lovely babies, Clucky, and you don't have to worry about being cooked now. The next time you decide you want to have a family, I'll ask Grandpa to bring his eggs back."

Jenny's birthday was in March. Mother decided that she would knit a bed jacket for her to wear when the baby came. She finished it the night before Jenny's birthday, which was on the Saturday.

The next morning as we were eating breakfast, we heard a quick knocking on the back door. Before mother could stand up the door opened, and Aunty Em rushed in.

"Can't stop. Jenny has a baby girl. Born at three o'clock this morning."

"That's wonderful," Mother cried.

"Can I come to see the baby?" I pleaded with Aunt Em. "We've got a present for Jenny's birthday. It's for her to wear in bed."

"Not 'til this afternoon, Katie. Jenny is sleeping now," said Aunt Em.

"Of course she is," said Mother. "We've got something else to do this morning Katie."

"Right," said Aunt. "I must get back before the baby wakes." And she hurried out again the way she had come.

"What have we got to do this morning, Mummy?"

"Find something for the baby. I still have your baby clothes, and I am sure some of them will fit Jenny's baby."

"Can I give the baby something?"

"When we have put together some clothes, we'll go to the store and find something. Come on. Help me choose some clothes for her."

I followed Mother up the stairs to her bedroom where she opened the wardrobe and took down a cardboard box from the shelf. She put it on the bed and I climbed up and sat beside it. Mother tore paper tape from the top of the box and opened the flaps. Inside were pink dresses and matinee jackets, blankets, and a white shawl. Mother took them out one by one, smiling at each item and occasionally gently holding a dress or jacket to her cheek. She laid them all out on the bed and said, "Which ones do you think Jenny will like?"

I picked a pretty pink dress with rosebuds embroidered around the hem and a matching jacket, a white and pink blanket, and the shawl.

Mother said, "Very good choices but I am sure Aunty Em has knitted the baby a shawl. Your grandmother knitted this for you. You might like to use it for a baby one day."

She picked up another dress and jacket and a pretty cotton bonnet with ribbons to tie under the baby's chin. These she added to the ones I chose. "There, I think that will do." She replaced the other things in the box and put it back in the closet. "Now we will find some pretty paper in my paper drawer to wrap them in. Then we'll go to the store for you to buy a gift."

We went to a store that sold nothing but baby things. I wandered around, looking at the silver cups and spoons, tiny shoes and socks, rattles and toys. It was very hard to choose. In the end, I decided to get a soft little bear. He had a large pink ribbon around his neck and felt very cuddly.

Mother paid the lady behind the counter for my bear and we went home to lunch.

It seemed to take forever for Mother to eat her lunch and wash up afterwards. I dried the dishes to speed things up but she still did not get ready to go. I did not wrap my bear because I knew the baby would not be able to unwrap it, and I waited impatiently for Mother to say we could go. The hand on the clock seemed to have stopped moving but at long last, mother put on her cardigan, picked up the parcel and her purse and said, "Okay, we can go now."

I ran and skipped ahead of mother so that she had to trot to keep up with me.

"Wait for me, Katie," she called. "I don't want you banging on Auntie's door and waking Jenny or the baby."

Bouncing from one foot to the other, I waited for her to reach aunt's house. She tapped gently on the door and opened it. Aunt Em came hurrying to meet us.

"Jenny's still sleeping," she whispered. "Come in. I'll go and fetch the baby."

She hurried off again and came back in a few minutes, carrying a basket. She put it down on the sofa and I leaned over to see the baby.

She was wrapped up in a shawl like the one I had seen that morning, and all I could see was a tiny, pink face and a fringe of fine, blonde hair. Her eyes were closed but every now and then her mouth moved as though she was sucking. I wished she would wake up.

I heard Aunt Em say something to Mother, who leant over me and said very quietly, "I am going to have a cup of tea with Aunty in the kitchen, but you can stay and watch the baby."

I nodded and watched them walking into the kitchen. Mother put her arm around Aunt and Aunt leaned her head on Mother's shoulder. It looked strange.

I wondered if I would be allowed to hold the baby if she woke up. I leaned close to her face and whispered, *"Bye baby Bunting, Daddy's gone a-hunting. Gone to get a rabbit skin, to wrap poor baby Bunting in."* Suddenly one eye opened. It was bright blue. I was so surprised that I stepped back. The other eye opened and for a moment it looked as though they were looking straight at me. Then as suddenly as they had opened, the eyes closed.

I was so excited I ran to the kitchen. "The baby opened her eyes," I cried.

Mother and Aunt Em stopped talking. They seemed surprised to see me.

"That's nice Katie." Mother stood up. "We'd better be going now."

"But we haven't said happy birthday to Jenny yet," I objected.

Mother put her finger to her lips. "Sh!" "Don't shout. Jenny's sleeping. She doesn't want visitors right now. We'll come back tomorrow. Give her our presents when she wakes, Em."

"I'm giving the baby my present now." I ran to the table and snatched the bear. "I'll put it in the basket."

"Yes, that's fine," said aunt. "Thank you Katie. She'll love it."

Mother hugged aunt and we left her sitting at the table, head in hands. As we walked down the path, I looked back and I was sure that the curtain in the front room flicked open and shut. We walked home in silence.

When we got in the house, I went upstairs and lay on my bed. Mother did not seem to care about the baby at all and Aunt Em was miserable. Well if they did not want to be bothered with the baby, I would look after her.

I heard Mother coming up the stairs. I grabbed a book from beside my bed and pretended to be reading. Mother knocked at the door. "May I come in, Katie?"

"I s'pose so," I mumbled grudgingly.

Mother sat on the bed. "I'm sorry if Aunty and I seemed a bit down. I'm afraid I have something to tell you that is very sad."

Now I was alarmed. "Is something wrong with Jenny?"

"No, no Jenny will be fine and the baby is all right. It's Arthur. After Aunty left us this morning, a telegram came for Jenny. Arthur was killed when his plane crashed over the sea."

"No, no, he can't be killed!" I cried. I flung myself at mother and she cradled me in her arms. "The baby has to have a daddy," I moaned between sobs, "and Jenny will be alone like Aunt Em."

"Yes, I know. It will be hard, but you and I, and Aunt Em will take care of Jenny and the baby. Right now, Jenny's hurting too much to see people. We'll go and see her in the morning when she may be feeling a little better."

That night, we prayed for Jenny and the baby and Aunt Em and all the mothers and babies who were hoping the war would end soon.

The next day, Mother and I went round to aunt's house to see Jenny.

"How's Jenny this morning?" Mother asked when aunt opened the door.

"As well as can be expected. Come in. I told her you would be round and she wants to see you. Especially Katie."

I pushed past Mother and ran into the front room. Jenny was sitting up in bed with the baby in her arms.

I rushed to her and put my arms around her. "Oh Jenny, I am so sad for you."

"Careful Katie. You'll squash me." I let go of her and saw that she was smiling. "I am very sad too, but I haven't lost Arthur completely. There is some of him in this little love." She gently stroked the baby's cheek. Mother and Aunty were standing in the doorway. Jenny looked at them. "That is why I am calling her Joy. She has brought me joy in a time of great sadness."

Mother and Aunt Em both rushed to the bed and kissed Jenny. They were crying and laughing at the same time.

"I think we could all use a cup of tea," said Aunt, wiping her eyes on her handkerchief.

"Yes, let's have a cup of tea," said Mother and Jenny at the same time. They looked at one another and laughed.

"It may be weak and not very sweet, but a cup of tea cures many ills," said Mother. "Now let me hold my great-niece."

I let out a sigh of relief. Adults behaved strangely sometimes, but most of the time they were pretty good.

Chapter 12

A couple of weeks later, a letter came from Helen to tell us that she was coming home on leave. She was arriving on Saturday, and going back to camp the following Wednesday. I was so excited I couldn't concentrate on anything Mrs Wilkins said at school. On Friday, Mother gave me a note to give to her. It said that I would not be in school on Monday and Tuesday because my sister was coming home.

Mrs Wilkins glared at me over the letter. "Judging by the way you were behaving last week, I do not suppose it will make any difference if you are here or not."

On Saturday morning, I was up and dressed at six o'clock. I ran to Mother's room and jumped on her bed. "Wake up Mummy, wake up. Helen is coming today."

Mother groaned and opened her eyes. "Good morning to you too Katie. Helen won't be here until tonight."

"I know but we have to be ready to go to meet her," I protested.

"I don't think we will be meeting her. She'll be coming on the Underground and I don't know what time to expect her. She knows the way home from the tube."

"But Mummy..."

"Katie please. I need my sleep. Helen might be very late and I want to be awake when she arrives."

Poor mother. I slipped off the bed and crept from the room. Downstairs, I made a jam sandwich for myself and wondered how I was going to survive until Helen came home.

I decided to decorate the kitchen and went to the cupboard under the stairs to find the crepe paper garlands we used at Christmas. Then I found some pieces of paper and used my crayons to write, WELCOME HOME HELEN on them. When Mother came downstairs she said, "That's nice. We'll put it on the living room door. It will be too dark for her to see it on the front door."

After she had eaten, Mother helped me arrange the garlands and we tidied the mess I had managed to make. Mother suggested that I dust the furniture to get rid of the "ants in your pants. You're making me tired just watching you," she complained. "Why don't you make a card for Helen? She can take it back to camp and look at it when she is feeling homesick."

Making the card kept me occupied until lunchtime, while Mother swept and tidied and made up Helen's bed. She put all the hot water bottles in the bed to make sure that the mattress was not damp.

After lunch, I went to play with Vicky and Violet so that Mother could have a rest. She sometimes complained that she was too old to have a small child running around her all day. Helen was born when Mother was twenty-eight and my birth twelve years later must have been a shock to her. As a child, I was aware that my mother was older than the mothers of most of the other children I knew, but this did not bother me. Mother loved me but the added responsibilities she had without my father around, worrying about him, Helen and me, and her job, had taken their toll. When the government evacuated children living in the cities to the country, I could have gone, but when Mother saw the list of things I would be allowed to take with me in my suitcase, she said that no child of hers would have to live with such a meagre wardrobe. I could take one vest, a pair of knickers, one petticoat, two pairs of stockings, six handkerchiefs, one long vest with shoulder straps, one blouse, one cardigan, an overcoat or mackintosh, a comb, one pair of Wellington boots, a towel, soap, facecloth, toothbrush, boots or shoes, and plimsolls (rubber-soled shoes with laced, canvas uppers). I suspect the real reason was that mother would not let me go to a place and people she did not know. I was shy with strangers and very glad to stay home.

During the Blitz, when the bombs were falling day and night, I did not go to school. I loved listening to the programmes for schools on the radio. It was much more fun listening to stories about historical events than copying and memorizing lists of the dates of the kings of England. There were even programmes for exercising to music. One day, the School Board man came to the house and asked why I was not in school. Mother replied, "She'll go back to school when Hitler stops dropping bombs in the daytime." However, when the bombing eased a little, Mother did let me go back. Perhaps she was tired of having me at home twenty-four hours a day. She wrote a note to the teacher explaining my absence, which Mrs Wilkins put in her desk drawer without reading it. Nothing was said about my absence.

This evening, Mother let me wait up in my pyjamas for Helen to come home. We were both excited but I was soon yawning and fighting to keep my eyes open. At some point, I lost the battle and the next thing I knew I was on Mother's lap and she was gently shaking me saying, "Wake up. Helen is at the door."

As Mother stood me on my feet, I heard the front door opening and mother ran to the hall. I followed and found her hugging Helen, with the light from the living room streaming out through the still-open front door. I hurried to shut the door before a warden saw the light and then wriggled my way between Helen and mother. Helen untangled herself from Mother and picked me up.

"My goodness, you're getting heavy. You must have grown," she said. "Let's go into the living room where I can see you properly."

She put me down and I pointed to the banner on the door.

"I love it," Helen said, kissing the top of my head.

Mother went into the kitchen to make tea and Helen followed her saying, "I must wash my hands." I went to the kitchen too determined not to miss a minute with Helen. I was now wide-awake.

As Helen turned on the tap, I noticed that her hands were very dirty. The water ran black as she soaped and rinsed them.

"What is all that dirt?" I asked.

Helen laughed. "Wait till Mum has made the tea and we are sitting down, and I'll tell you," she said.

"Are you hungry Helen?" mother asked.

"No, I had something to eat at Waterloo Station before I got on the tube."

Mother poured three cups of tea, mine mostly milk, and put a few biscuits on a small plate. "We haven't got much in the way of goodies, I'm afraid," she said.

"That reminds me. While I am here, you can use my ration book as well as your own," said Helen. "You can't be expected to feed three people with two people's rations."

"We might as well sit in the kitchen to drink our tea," mother suggested.

Helen sat in her usual place at the table and mother and I sat either side of her.

I watched Helen drink some of her tea and take a bite of her biscuit. I couldn't wait any longer to hear what had made her hands so dirty.

"We're sitting down. Now will you tell us why your hands were black?" I pleaded.

Helen went out to the hall and came back with the bag she had left there. She opened it and pulled out a piece of knitting on two needles. "This is the beginning of a jumper for you, Katie. I unpicked an old one of mine that had a hole in it."

"Thank you," I said. "But what's that got to do with your dirty hands?"

Helen plunged her hands into the bag and pulled out a large bundle of tangled yarn. It was as black as Helen's hands had been.

"Goodness gracious, what happened to that? It's black as Newgate's knocker," Mother exclaimed.

"Well," said Helen. "I was knitting on the tube train and when we came above ground, the lights went out because of the blackout. The train was crowded with people crushed together in the aisles and between the doors. The train jerked to a sudden stop between stations and my ball of wool fell off my lap. I tried to pick it up, but in the darkness I couldn't find it. The train started again and travelled to the next station. The doors opened and people began to move toward them to get off the train. As they went, they took my wool with them. Then other people got onto the train and they too became tangled up in the wool. Some of them turned on torches and in their light, I saw my ball of wool disappearing out of the train's closing door. Those who had wool around their feet and ankles were desperately trying to get rid of it. They looked as if they were doing some strange dance. A man in army uniform just inside the door was frantically pulling the yarn back into the train. I tried to tell him not to bother but he kept on pulling. By now the ball must have been bouncing along the track beneath the train. The standing passengers were still doing an imitation of St. Vitus' Dance and getting more and more tangled. I was mortified and apologizing profusely."

By this time, mother and I were laughing until we cried.

Helen continued. "At the next station, the man at the doors managed to pull up the remainder of the wool and breaking it off at the first foot he came across, handed it to me. I thanked him again and again and he said, 'You can't waste wool these days, miss. It'll be fine after you wash it.' I hurriedly stuffed the bundle in my bag. One by one, the hog-tied passengers managed to untangle themselves. 'I beg your pardon,' 'Whoops,' and the occasional swear word could be heard in the darkness. Everyone was remarkably sympathetic, and some, when they left the train, even handed me the wool that had been tangled around their legs and feet. I spent the rest of the journey apologising and wishing that I could leave the train without being seen. I'll never knit on a train again!"

Helen looked so downcast that mother and I tried to stop laughing and commiserate with her, but soon the three of us were giggling hysterically and I was rolling about on the floor. It was some minutes before we all calmed down.

"Oh my," said mother, who by this time was crying with laughter and dabbing her eyes with her handkerchief. "I can't remember laughing that hard since the war started. That laugh has done me a world of good. In fact I feel so good that I'll volunteer to wash the wool for you."

"Thanks Mum. You don't have to do that. I'll do it in the morning. I think that right now my bed is calling. Let's get a good night's sleep, so we'll have lots of energy tomorrow."

"Suits me fine," said Mother. "Come along Katie, and try not to wake me at six tomorrow morning."

The next morning, I slept until nine o'clock. Mother and Helen were already in the kitchen eating toast and jam. I joined them and mother made some more toast.

"What are we going to do today?" I asked, spluttering toast crumbs over the tablecloth.

"Katie, don't talk with your mouth full. It's rude and look at the mess you've made."

"Oh Mum," said Helen. "She's excited."

"That's no reason to eat like a pig."

I hung my head. "Sorry Mummy," I said.

"I should think so," was mother's response.

Helen glanced at me and grinned. "I am going to wash that dirty wool, and then we can take my ration book to the shops and see what we can buy for dinner. How's that?"

"That's good," I said. "I'll help you wash the wool."

"Let me wash the dishes first," said Mother.

"No Mum, I'll wash the dishes and Katie will dry them, won't you Katie?"

"Yes," I cried and picked up my plate and carried it to the sink.

Mother cleared the table and Helen filled the bowl in the sink with water. "Now Mum, you sit down and read the newspaper. You should write a list of the food you need too."

"Thanks Helen. You too Katie. I'm sorry I lost my temper with you. I just feel that all the things that used to make life pleasant are forgotten these days."

She gave me a hug and I said, "It's all right Mum."

The dishes were soon put away and Helen fetched the bundle of wool and dumped it in clean water in the sink. She scrubbed it with soap and we both squeezed it until the water was black and the wool turned blue. Then Helen changed the water several times until it ran clear.

"Okay that'll do. Let's take this to the garden and hang it on the clothes line." She carried the bowl of wool and I followed, carrying the peg bag. Helen took the peg bag and hung it on the line. "You hold the bowl please, Katie, and I'll try to hang the wool over the line."

Getting it on the line was not easy. Helen grabbed a handful of wool in each hand and shook the wet bundle above the bowl. Water sprayed over both of us and I stepped back, causing the bowl to tip and pour water over Helen's feet. Helen jumped back, and all the wool came out of the bowl and dripped even more water onto the ground, and both our feet. Helen got the wool back into the bowl and tried again to loop some of it over the line. This time she succeeded, and holding the wool in place, fumbled in the peg bag for a peg. She repeated this manoeuvre. At last, all the wool was drooping along the clothesline, anchored in place by a plethora of pegs. Water continued to drip along the length of the line.

Helen breathed out in a long sigh. "I think that will have to do," she said. "Come on, let's go in and get ourselves dry. Then we'll go to the shops."

Mother collected her purse, shopping basket, and a list of things she wanted to buy, and off we went to the High Street. Helen was surprised at the small amounts of food we could buy with our coupons, even with the added allowance to cover her leave.

"How do you manage, Mum?" she asked.

"Oh we don't do too badly. We have vegetables and lots of fruit in the garden. I think we probably eat a better diet with less sugar. The children have extra milk and coupons to give them a few candies. We can still buy fish and chips. There aren't oranges in the shops very often, and when a delivery of bananas comes in, there are long line-ups at the lucky shop, even though they can only be bought for children younger than five years old."

"I miss ice-cream," I added, "and ice cream sodas and I don't much like the candies they have in the shops. But I like powdered eggs."

"Powdered eggs? Oh no! Not those horrible powdered eggs," said Helen, shuddering and screwing her face into a terrible grimace. "We have them in the camp."

"You look how I feel about them," mother laughed, "but I only use them for baking now we have the chickens. Tomorrow, in your honour, I'll make real eggs scrambled for breakfast and remind you of what real eggs taste like."

In the butcher's, Mother bought some neck of lamb. "That will make a nice Irish stew with dumplings and barley," she said. I felt my mouth begin to water at the thought. The meat ration was one shilling and two pence-worth of meat for one person per week, and neck of lamb was the cheapest meat one could buy, but it was really good when made into Irish Stew.

On the way home, I saw a young boy coming toward us carrying a cloth-covered basket over his arm. As he drew nearer, I thought I could hear mewing sounds coming from beneath the cloth. I ran toward him and asked, "What have you got there?"

"Kittens," replied the boy. "I'm taking them to the pet store."

I turned and ran back toward Mother and Helen, calling as I went. "Mummy, Mummy, there's a boy in the street with a basket of kittens. He's taking them to the pet shop to sell. Could we buy one?"

Mother frowned. "I don't know if that is a good idea, Katie. We might not be able to feed it."

"Oh please, Mummy," I begged, hugging her around the waist.

"Do you remember what Daddy said?"

"Yes but..."

Helen looked at Mother. "Would a little kitten eat so much?"

"Don't you start," Mother said, half grinning and half scowling at Helen.

"Let's just look at them, eh?" Helen winked at me.

By now, the boy had passed us and I was anxiously jiggling from one foot to the other. Mother looked after the boy. "Oh all right. We're just looking though."

Helen called out and ran after the boy. He turned and walked back to us. Mother lifted the cloth and we all peered into the basket. Five small balls of fur wriggled and jiggled about on a blanket.

"Oh, Mum," Helen sighed. "They're adorable." She picked one up and held it against her cheek. Then she held it to my face, and all the sadness I had felt over the loss of my pets overcame me again. Tears ran down my cheeks.

Mother put down her basket. "All right. I know when I'm outnumbered." She took the kitten from Helen, turned it onto its back, and studied it. Shaking her head, she replaced it in the basket and picked up another one. She examined this one in the same way and put that one back in the basket. Two more suffered the same fate. I was getting worried. When the fifth one had been looked over and replaced, my heart fell to my feet. Mother turned to me. "Which would you like, a black one or a tabby?"

For a moment, I could not believe what I had heard. "You mean I can have one?" I stammered.

"Oh for goodness sake. Yes you may have one, just one. Look," she pulled me to the basket and pointed at the kittens. "There's the black one and there's the tabby. Which one do you want?"

I looked at the two kittens with longing. I had to choose one and that was not going to be easy. I picked up the tabby and it began to wriggle and squeal, trying to get out of my hand. I quickly put it down and gently disentangled the black one from the squirming bundle. This one gave one little squeak and opened the bluest eyes I had ever seen. "This one Mummy, please."

"Good," said Mother. "How much do you want for it?" she asked the boy.

"Dunno," said the boy. "I was going to sell them as one bunch."

Mother looked in her purse and brought out a coin. "Here's a shilling. Is that enough?"

The boy shrugged. "I s'pose so. Thanks." And replacing the cloth over the basket, he went on his way.

"Good choice," said Helen. "Now we have to name it. Is it a male or a female?' she asked Mother. "I assume you know which it is, since you examined it."

"It's a tom. There were only two."

"How do you know its name is Tom?" I asked.

Helen laughed. "Oh Katie. Male cats are called tomcats. I don't really know why."

"Oh. Why did you only want a male cat, Mummy?"

"Because a male can't have more baby kittens to feed."

"How did you know it was a male?" I asked.

"He had a winkle."

I was none the wiser. Having no brother, I had never seen a penis. I decided I should stop while I was ahead. I had my kitten and it did not matter whether it was a boy or a girl. If I had not had a kitten to hold, I would have skipped the rest of the way home.

When we had our tea, the kitten slurped from a saucer of milk. Then he curled up on a piece of blanket mother had provided and fell asleep.

"What name are you going to give him?" Helen asked me.

"I don't know. Blackie maybe."

"That's not very imaginative," mother ventured.

"I know what his name should be," said Helen. "Mum paid the boy a shilling for him, so why don't you call him Bob?"

"That's a good idea," said mother.

Bob was the name we gave to the shilling coin.

I knelt beside the kitten and stroked his head. He drowsily opened his eyes and stretched. "Shall we call you Bob? Do you like that name, kitten?" I asked. A small, pink tongue popped out and licked my hand. "Yes, he likes his name," I informed Helen and Mother.

That night, Bob slept on my bed and the only sound I heard as I fell asleep was his gentle purrs.

The rest of Helen's leave passed quickly. Mother took two days off from work on Monday and Tuesday, and on Tuesday evening, we made the trip to the train station once more, to see her safely on her way. The clean wool was stowed at the bottom of Helen's bag. "I'll start knitting again when I get back to camp," she said. "I'm not risking a repeat of the ball of wool tango on the train again."

When someone was in the forces they did not have holidays or days off duty. Helen could request a pass for twenty four hours leave or longer if there was a reason for needing it or her senior officer felt that the situation was such that her being out of the camp for a day or two would not cause any problems. This would only happen infrequently and sometimes I did not see her for several months at a time. Before she was called up she would take me to the park at weekends or to see a movie. To me a few months seemed like a lifetime.

Chapter 13

The summer came and went. In July sweets and chocolate were rationed to one ounce per person per week, and cookies were rationed in August.

Also in August, a second attempt to invade Europe was made. The British and Canadian forces and a small group of U.S. Rangers landed on the beaches of Dieppe. It was another disaster. The Canadians especially suffered enormous losses. More than 3,000 Canadians died or were taken prisoner. It was thought that the Germans had learned of the attack before it happened.

Jenny went back to work and Joy was looked after during the day in a nursery run by the Council. Occasionally Jenny and Aunt Em would go to the cinema in the evening, and Mother and I babysat Joy.

I loved watching Jenny get ready to go out. Stockings were included in the Clothing Ration Book, and silk stockings had disappeared along with oranges and bananas. Jenny painted her legs with a special brown paint to look like stockings. Real stockings had a seam down the back. "It makes your legs look good," Jenny explained. When she had painted her legs, she then took a darker brown pencil and carefully drew a line from her ankle to above her hemline. This was tricky because she had to twist her body round to do it. The left leg was the hardest to get straight and that was where I was allowed to help. Concentrating hard, I would slowly draw the pencil up Jenny's leg. Jenny would start giggling and this made it even harder to keep the line straight.

"Jenny stop wiggling. You'll have a crooked seam," I would cry in frustration.

"I can't help it. It tickles when you do it. I don't know why. It doesn't when I do it myself."

"For goodness sake," Aunty would complain as she pushed Jenny out of the house. "Stop fussing and get going. We'll be late for the film. Nobody's going to see your legs in the cinema."

As soon as they had gone, I would go and sit beside Joy's crib and hope that she woke up. Sometimes she did, and Mother let me nurse her back to sleep. They were the best times.

Chapter 14

Some children had very sweet teeth and the rationing of sweets hit them hard. Vicky and Violet Davis loved sweets. When the government rationed sweets to three ounces a week, they were really upset. I didn't like the hard candies that seemed to be the only kind in the sweet shop, so mother would sometimes exchange my sweet coupons for tea. She could always rely on trading sweet coupons with Vicky and Violet's mother.

One Saturday morning, as mother and I were clearing away the breakfast dishes, Vicky and Violet appeared at the kitchen door. I let them in.

"Hello Katie, morning Mrs Wells," Vicky said. "Mum said, would you like to exchange some tea and sugar coupons for some candy coupons? Violet and I have used all ours."

Mother laughed. "It's a good job Katie doesn't like boiled sweets, isn't it? Your sweet teeth would be very unhappy. Yes I would love some extra tea and sugar."

She went to her purse and pulled out my ration book. "Here you are, the last two. You've used all the others."

Vicky handed over the tea and sugar coupons and mother put them in her book.

"Do you want to come to the shop with us, Katie?" asked Vicky.

"Yes, you go along," said mother. You'll only sit around here moping otherwise."

"Okay," I said. I went to the hall closet to get my coat and shoes. The sweetshop was just around the corner. It was a small shop that also sold newspapers, comics, and magazines. It was called, "Sweets for Sweets," because the owner was Mrs Sweet. She was a little, round lady with rosy cheeks and a bright smile for every child who came through her door.

The shop windows were taped, which made the inside of the shop dark. A single twenty-five-watt light bulb over the counter provided enough light for Mrs Sweet to read her weigh scales and cash register.

"Hello there," she said as Vicky, Violet and I opened the door and set the bell over it ringing. "I didn't expect to see you two again until next month. I thought you had eaten your ration last week."

"Yes, Mrs Sweet, we did, but Katie doesn't like boiled sweets and she always has coupons over."

"Well, I think it is very nice of her to let you have them. What do you want today?"

Vicky looked at Violet. "Shall we have the lemon or the raspberry?" she asked.

"Raspberry," said Violet.

Vicky gave the coupons to Mrs Sweet, who took a large glass jar of violent-red, boiled candies from the shelf behind her. She weighed out a few sweets into the scale and then poured them into a paper cone.

While she was doing this, the doorbell tinkled again. Vicky looked round to see who had come in, and gasped. I turned to see what had surprised her. I saw a man in the light-blue uniform of the RAF, standing just inside the shop. He wore gloves on his hands, but it was his face that had caused Vicky to gasp. As he walked farther into the light, I could see that one side of his face was red and puckered and he had only half a nose and no eyebrows or eyelashes.

Mrs Sweet looked up and her face broke into an enormous smile. She dropped the bag of sweets and ran out from behind the counter. "Billy!" she cried, and flung herself into the man's arms.

When they parted, I could see that while Mrs Sweet was still smiling, there were tears running down her cheeks. "Children I'm sorry. I'll give you your sweets. This is my son. His plane was shot down and he has been in the hospital."

Billy smiled as well as he could with his puckered lips. "I hope I didn't give you too much of a fright," he said. "I never was the handsomest bloke in town, but having me plane burst into flames didn't improve me much. At least people notice me now." He fumbled one gloved hand into his pocket and pulled out something. He nodded at Violet, who had taken shelter behind Vicky and was peeping out from behind her back. "Come 'ere littl'un. I don't bite. My officer gave me this bar of chocolate for being a good boy. You can 'ave it if you like."

Vicky pushed Violet towards Billy. She went forward until she could reach the chocolate, and then quickly scampered back to the protection of her big sister.

"What d'you say to Billy?" Vicky prompted.

"Thank you, sir."

"Yes, thank you," Vicky and I said together.

I did not know where to look. I knew it was rude to stare, but it seemed unkind not to look at Billy Sweet. The three of us made to leave the shop but were stopped by Mrs Sweet.

"Here, don't forget your sweets," she called and handed the small bag across the counter. "Now Billy, come to the back and I'll make you a nice cup of tea."

"Goodbye kids," said Billy.

"Goodbye and thank you," we called back as we hurried through the door, setting the bell jingling once more.

Outside, Vicky took the bar of chocolate from Violet. "I'll divide it into three," she said, taking off the wrapping.

Violet watched carefully to make sure that the pieces were all the same size. Vicky held the three pieces on her hand. "Here, I divided, so you choose," she said to Violet and me. Violet quickly snatched a piece and crammed it into her mouth.

Vicky and I laughed. "You'll be sick," Vicky warned. "I'm going to save mine. You'll be sorry when I'm enjoying my piece and you don't have any left."

I took the third piece and put it in my pocket. "I'll share mine with Mummy after dinner." I sighed. "Before the war, Daddy used to buy us chocolates."

Chapter 15

1943 A NEW SCHOOL

The entry of the United States into the war, in June, had turned the tide at last in our favour. Air raids happened less frequently, and to mother's relief, sausages were rationed. Her battles with exploding sausages became fewer. One item of food that was not rationed was bread, so even the small amount of meat that had been put in sausages must have become even less.

Since Clucky had raised her first batch of chicks, she had spent more time sitting on china eggs than laying real ones. By the time I had twelve hens laying, I was able to sell eggs to the neighbours. By the time Christmas came in 1942, I had twenty-four hens and Grandpa built another hen house and run for me. Although I could only sell my customers their ration allowance, the money I got for the eggs paid for the chicken feed and straw and left a small amount of cash for me to spend. Mother helped me with the forms the government needed when I sent in the ration coupons for their records. There was not much to spend the earnings on, so I opened a Post Office Savings Account and soon had what mother called, "a nice little nest egg," which was a very appropriate name for it. I hoped the day that I could spend it would come soon.

The chickens kept me busy, but I found time to write to father when mother did. Sometimes we did not hear from him for weeks, and then the letters were short and often had passages blacked out by the censorship officials. Mother explained that this was done so that if the enemy got hold of the letter, it would not give away any secrets. I did not think father would know any secrets, but I supposed he might mention something he had done or a place he had visited that seemed unimportant to him but could be very important to the enemy. The censor made sure that we never knew exactly where father was.

We could never forget that we were fighting a war. Every newsreel at the cinema showed fighting in Europe or the Far East, bombs dropping on towns, and cities and refugees plodding in one direction along foreign roads, their possessions on their backs or in hand-held carts, and tanks and soldiers marching on the same roads in the opposite direction. All around us, posters told us to, "Dig For Victory," "Waste Not–Want Not," "Make Do And Mend," "Look Out In The Blackout," or warned that "Careless Talk Costs Lives." "Is Your Journey Really Necessary?" was itself not really necessary. Few people travelled far, unless they had to. In case we were invaded by the enemy, all the railway station place names and signposts on the roads had been removed. It made travelling away from home like a mystery tour.

1943 was a very important year for me because I had to sit my eleven plus exam. If I passed, I would go to a grammar school where I would stay until I could take my university entrance exam. If I failed, I would go to the Secondary School and go to work at fourteen. There were five grammar schools in the area and we could choose which one we preferred to go to. I had chosen the one that Mother and Helen had gone to. Vicky decided to go to that one too.

The exam was taken in June and I had to stay at school all day, because there were exams in the morning and afternoon. I could not go home to lunch and had to eat at the school. Some children whose mothers worked too far from home to be there to give them lunch, had eaten school lunches all through the war. When I was served my school lunch, I was glad that I had not had to eat at school every day. We had soggy green cabbage with watery mashed potatoes and some kind of ground-up meat floating in brown water. Yech!

The results began to come to the school about two weeks later. They did not all come at once. One day, several children might be told that they had passed and been accepted by their chosen school, the next, only one might get good news.

A week went by and neither my name nor Vicky's had been called by the teacher. At the beginning of the second week, I listened anxiously to the names of the children and the schools they were going to and realised that the school I wanted to go to had not been mentioned. Thinking about it, I could not remember hearing my school's name being called out any day. What if the school had taken all its children from other elementary schools? If I had passed the exam, I would be put in a grammar school, but if it was not the one I wanted, I would be very upset.

On Tuesday, Vicky's name was called. She looked at me and crossed her fingers. The teacher read the name of the school. It was not the one we had chosen. My name was not called. Vicky shrugged. At least she had passed. Maybe I hadn't. On the walk home I told her, "Well done, Vicky. It's a shame you didn't get the school you wanted."

"Oh I don't really care. My mum and dad didn't go to grammar school. But I'm sorry we'll be going to different schools."

"Yes, I'm sorry too. It looks as though I might be going to the secondary school."

"Nah, you'll pass and I bet you'll go to the school you want." She slapped me on the back and crossed the road to her house. "See you after lunch."

"Yes, see you."

Mother had stopped asking me if I knew which school I would be going to. I think she was as anxious as I was. She insisted that it did not matter if I did not go to grammar school, but I knew it would. Father would be disappointed too. If I had failed the exam, I would be too ashamed to tell him.

The next morning I sat at my desk, feeling miserable. There were only about ten children who had not heard yet, and most of them were not expected to pass the exam. The teacher looked at the paper on which the day's results were written.

She looked around the classroom.

"Jeremy, you have been accepted at Elworth Boy's School. Katie, you have been accepted at Springwood. Congratulations both of you."

I felt as though I was going to burst with happiness. I had passed the exam and I was going to my mother's old school. A great weight had been lifted from me. I felt light as air. I began writing my letter to Father in my head. Vicky caught my eye and smiled. "Told you," she mouthed, pointing at me. I smiled back and responded, "I wish you were coming with me. We'll still be friends."

The rest of the morning dragged along. I could not wait to get home to tell Mother my news.

In August, a letter came from the grammar school with a list of things I would need when I started school. I had to have a uniform; a blue tunic, a white blouse, blue blazer, blue beret with the school badge on it, black, lace-up shoes, long black socks, a pair of plimsolls, short dress for games and gym, and an apron for domestic science. Clothes were still rationed, so we were invited to the school to get uniforms that other children had grown out of. Mother and I went to the school on the evening given in the letter, and found the school hall crowded with other parents and children, all sorting through stacks of clothes laid out on wooden tables.

Some of the clothes were too big for me and some too small, but after about an hour, Mother and I had our arms full of things that more or less fit me. The school secretary sat at the door taking donations of money to be divided between the people who had provided the clothes.

Before we went home, teachers took groups of parents and children on tours of the school. The group Mother and I were in was led by a small, elderly gentleman. He wore a black gown over his clothes like the one a judge wears. It was dusty with chalk. He showed us where the science labs were; the art room; the fields where we would play field hockey, cricket, and rounders; England's version of baseball, and the tennis and netball courts. We would learn domestic science in a real cottage. In one of the small bedrooms, there was even a crib with a large baby doll in it. I pointed it out to Mother. "The doll is for teaching you how to bathe a baby," she whispered.

I was delighted with my new school: the labs with their long benches and high stools, Bunsen burners, and cupboards filled with glassware; the art room with high windows to let in the light and prints on the walls; the school fields; the gym with its ropes and wall bars to climb; and especially the little cottage with the baby in the crib. I felt that a whole new world had opened to me. No more Mrs Deane. I hoped Vicky's school was as nice as mine.

The second week in September, I woke early and put on my new second-hand uniform. I ran downstairs to show Mother. She was putting one of our own eggs in my eggcup for my breakfast, but she turned as I came into the kitchen.

She hugged me tight and then held me at arm's length. There were tears in her eyes. "Oh Katie," she said. "You look so grown up. I wish your Daddy could see you."

"So do I," I said. Now I was sad.

Mother put her arm around me. "I am sorry Katie. This is an important day for you. I don't mean to upset you. Tonight we'll write to Daddy, and tell him all about your first day at grammar school. He'll be so proud of you. Now eat your breakfast or you'll be late on your first day."

I was a little afraid when I got to the school. Some of the students were as big as adults and there was no one there that I knew. A bell rang and everyone began to pour into the building. Inside, one wall was covered with sheets of names. I found mine and saw that I was in Room-1. A girl beside me said, "Are you in Room-1?"

"Yes," I said.

"Oh good, I am too. Let's find it together."

We soon found Room-1. The teacher was sitting at her desk and told us to sit wherever we wanted. The girl and I sat in desks side by side.

"My name's Katie," I told her.

"Mine's Julie," said the girl. "Can we be friends?"

"Sure."

When all the desks were filled, the teacher stood up and introduced herself. "My name is Miss Williams. You will call me, ma'am. If you want to ask me anything, put up your hand and say, 'Please ma'am.' Understood?"

"Yes, ma'am," we all said in unison.

"Good," said Miss Williams. "I am your form teacher. Now I will explain to you about your other teachers."

I had never had 'other teachers' before. Miss Williams explained that she would not teach us anything. We would have other teachers for every subject. One for English, one for mathematics, one for science, one for art, one for geography, one for history, one for sports, one for domestic science, one for music and one for French. twelve plus Miss Williams! Miss Williams was handing out timetables.

"These tell you which teacher will be with you, for which period in the day. Every teacher except the art teacher, the science teacher, the domestic science teacher and the sports teacher will come to the classroom. Every morning, when the bell goes, you come to this room. Then I will lead you to the hall for morning assembly. After assembly, you will go to your first class. That will be this room unless you have art, biology, chemistry, physics, domestic science, music or sports in which case you will go to the appropriate classroom, laboratory or to the cottage. On the back of your timetable you will find a map of the school with all the classrooms marked so you should be able to find your way around. There is also a list of all your teachers so your homework for today will be to memorize that information.

If you are late getting to school, a prefect will meet you at the front door, take down your name, and you will be brought to the hall when the notices are being read out. The headmistress will explain everything else you need to know at assembly. We shall go there now. Follow me, in single file."

Miss Williams marched out of the room and we all leapt up and followed her. From all over the school, children were merging, in disciplined lines, on the hall where I had come to find my uniform. At one end, there was a stage on which were rows of chairs on each side, a piano, and a dais in the middle. The rest of the hall was filled with rows of chairs. As the teachers and children came in, some went up onto the stage and sat down; children one side, teachers the other. The teachers all wore black gowns over their other clothes, which made them look like rows of crows.

Miss Williams led us to sit in a row near the front. When all the chairs were filled, a small, prim lady entered the hall. This was the headmistress. Everyone stood up as she mounted the steps to the stage. She went to the dais and looked out at us.

"Good morning everyone. Let us pray."

Everyone bowed their heads and the headmistress said a prayer. We all said the Lord's Prayer and then sat down.

One of the teachers sitting on the stage moved to the piano and the children on the stage stood up. The piano played and the children sang a hymn. When they finished, the headmistress introduced herself, and after welcoming the new students, explained the rules of the school and what clubs we could join for after-school activities. By the time assembly was finished and we were walking back to the classroom, my head was spinning. How would I remember all this? I would certainly have a lot to write to father.

Mother was sympathetic when I told her about my day. "You'll soon get used to it. You'll see," she assured me. At the time, I doubted her but as the days passed, I did settle and was soon enjoying my new school. None of the teachers treated us the way Mrs Deane had. They made us feel more like adults. Vicky said things were the same at her school, so we still had things to talk about when our homework was done.

Chapter 16

1944 – 1945

DOODLEBUGS AND ROCKETS

The war dragged on for another two years. The planes no longer flew over, dropping bombs every night, and mother and I were able to sleep in our beds in the house again.

The last week in May, I developed a bad cough. My breathing became wheezy and I ran a temperature. Mother put me in bed and phoned our doctor to come to the house. He came after he finished morning surgery. His cold stethoscope on my chest and back made me shiver. After listening to my breathing and taking my temperature, he confirmed that I did have a fever and said he would make up some medicine for me and send it round to the house.

"What's wrong with her?" mother asked.

"She has congestion of the lungs. Never let her sleep in the air raid shelter again. There won't be any more planes dropping bombs on us. The war will be over soon."

Thanks to the doctor's medicine, I was able to get up and return to school in a couple of weeks. However, though he was right about there being no more planes dropping bombs he underestimated the ingenuity of the German scientists.

In June 1944, the V-1s, nicknamed Doodlebugs, appeared in the skies over England. These were motorized bombs that throbbed over the country until their motors gave out. No one could tell exactly where the bomb would go or when it would fall. The air raid warning went as soon as one was spotted over the coast, so it was sometimes many hours before the bomb fell. No one took to the shelters until a doodlebug was heard overhead. Then they would watch it until the engine stopped. If it was nearby, they ran to the shelters. Sometimes people forgot that the air raid warning had sounded until they heard the throb of the bomb's motor.

One day, this happened to Mother. The warning had gone before noon and later in the afternoon, when I came home from school, she asked me to go round to the bakers for a loaf of bread. She gave me the money and said, "Come straight back."

I ran down the road and around the corner to the bakery. The shop was crowded, so I had to wait in a queue to be served. It was several minutes before I reached the counter and was given a loaf of bread. I gave the shop girl the money and began to squeeze past the other people who were still waiting. When I reached the door and pulled it open, I heard the familiar sound of a Doodlebug throbbing along overhead. Everyone in the shop turned to listen to the sound. As I watched the sky, I saw the bomb slowly chugging along above the street. I stood frozen to the spot as it moved past the shop.

Suddenly the motor stopped. Someone grabbed me from behind and slammed the door shut. Everyone in the shop fell to the floor, hands over their heads.

For a moment there was silence, and then an enormous explosion came from somewhere close by. The shop shook and its windows rattled in the blast. I leapt up and rushed out of the shop. Clutching the loaf of bread to my chest, I ran as fast as my legs would carry me toward home. I rounded the corner like a whirlwind and banged into someone running just as hard in the opposite direction. I felt strong arms clutching me to a familiar bosom.

"Thank God, thank God," Mother cried between sobs. "Katie I am so sorry. I forgot about the air raid warning. Are you all right?"

I disentangled myself from Mother's arms and looked at the loaf, which was crushed and dropping bread crumbs all over me and Mother. I began to giggle. "Yes, I'm all right but the bread isn't. I saw the bomb going along the road. I wonder where it fell?"

"Too close," said mother taking the sad-looking loaf and putting her arm around my shoulder. "Too close for comfort. Come on, let's go home. We'll find out where it fell soon enough."

The next day we heard that the bomb had fallen on a school. Fortunately the children and staff had all gone home, so no one was hurt.

In September, a new weapon was hurled at Britain. V-2s or rockets arrived without warning. They were like giant fireworks that were shot across the English Channel, and I hated them more than the doodlebugs. Mother said that I should think of them as thunder. "If you hear the bang, you are all right," she explained.

I still jumped every time a rocket exploded. Sometimes, at the school morning assembly, the headmistress read out the name of a past Springwood student who had died in Europe, and we stood in silence for a minute in her honour.

These announcements made me realise that if the war did not end in a few years, I could be fighting somewhere in Europe. This brought the war closer than the bombs, doodlebugs, and rockets had. I found myself worrying about Father. Even when Arthur had been killed, I thought that nothing would happen to *my father*. I suppose that then I was too young to understand such things. Now that I was older, I did understand. Now I understood the stress that my mother and all the adults were under every day.

Chapter 17

All through these years, Clucky had been raising baby chicks. Grandfather had built a third hen house, and I had a long list of customers who bought eggs from me. Every Saturday morning, I cleaned out the nest boxes and replaced the straw. Then I put out my 'eggs for sale' note on the gate and served my customers.

Clucky no longer laid any eggs, but I would not let Grandfather kill her. "She has to keep an eye on all her great, great, great, great grandchicks," I explained.

Actually, Clucky was the only living thing that I could tell my worries to. She never told me, "Don't be silly," or, "There's nothing to worry about." Mother had enough worries of her own without my much less important ones. Clucky knew nothing of the war or its consequences any more than I had when I was younger. As long as I provided her with clean straw and food, she was happy.

There was one human being that could make me forget the war. Jenny's baby, Joy. She was two years old now. Like her name, she brought a smile to the face of everyone she met. I loved looking after her when Jenny wanted time to herself. Awake, she was a bubbly bundle of energy; asleep, the perfect example of pure relaxation. I hoped that she would grow up in a world where there was no war. If I had to fight for that, I would be glad to do so. That, I realised, was why my father was fighting; for me, Helen, and mother, and all the people he loved.

On May 8th, 1945, the war in Europe ended. Mothers all over Britain arranged street parties for the children. Mother and I helped string bunting and flags from one house to another, across the street. I wondered if these were the same flags that had been used when the First World War ended. I saved up the eggs from the chickens, and proudly gave them to Mother to make hard-boiled-egg sandwiches. My customers would have to do without their eggs this week.

On the day of the party, everyone was busy setting up long tables made of planks stretched across smaller tables. The houses were stripped of chairs for the children to sit on. The excitement grew, as plates of bread and jam, spam, and large bowls of jelly appeared. I had just put the last plate of egg sandwiches on a table, when I heard someone calling my name. I turned to see Jimmy and Dougie running down the street.

They were waving flags and whooping and hollering. I rushed to meet them. We collided on the street where the Kings' house had been, where now there was a large hole.

"Jimmy, Dougie, where did you come from?" I gasped as we danced around in a circle of joy.

"We've been living with our auntie," said Dougie. He saw one of his friends and ran off.

"Your mum told us about the party and said we could come," Jimmy explained. "Mum brought us on the bus. She's over there talking to your mum." Jimmy nodded in the direction of my house. "Have you got a kitten yet?"

"Yes, and I've got a lot of chickens. Come and see them."

I led him to the back garden and the chicken houses, and told him the long story of Clucky's life.

Jimmy was impressed. "Gee, do you think she knew it was Christmas Eve when she laid that egg?"

"I like to think she did," I said. "If she hadn't laid an egg, you wouldn't be getting egg sandwiches at the party."

"Made with *real* eggs?" asked Jimmy, round-eyed.

"Yes," I said. "Let's go and get a seat near one of my plates so we're sure to get one."

My egg sandwiches disappeared faster than snow at the equator. When all the plates were empty, the children were seated on the road and the grandfather of a child from the next street did some magic tricks for us. While we were being entertained, the mothers cleared the chairs, tables, plates, and bowls away. We clapped and cheered when the magician pulled a rabbit from a top hat and took his final bow. "I wonder how that rabbit escaped becoming Sunday dinner?" I whispered in Jimmy's ear. The end of the show was the cue for the mothers to put some records on a gramophone and everyone began to dance.

When the sun went down, there was another surprise. The lamplighter came down the street on his bicycle, and winding between the children, turned on the streetlights with a long pole. Some of the younger children had never seen the streetlights lit, and they stared in awe at the gas lights as they flickered into life. When he left the lamplighter was cheered on his way to the next street.

It got dark and the adults still danced in the street. Babies slept in the arms of grandmothers and one by one, the older children were taken off to bed.

Jimmy, Dougie and I were playing hopscotch under the street lamp when our mothers came to find us. "It's time to go home, boys," said Mrs King.

We groaned. "Can't we stay a bit longer?" asked Jimmy.

"No, we'll miss the last bus if we don't go. I have promised Katie's mother that we'll come and visit another day, so come along now. Say goodbye to Katie."

"Bye, Katie," Jimmy and Dougie mumbled.

"Thanks for the egg sandwiches," said Jimmy. "We'll come again soon and p'raps you'll be able to visit us when we get our own place to live."

"Oh yes, I will. I have missed you. Goodbye Mrs King. Goodbye Jimmy, Dougie."

Mrs King gave Mother a hug. "Thank you so much for letting us know about the party. I wish we could come back here." She looked at the cleared space where her house had been. "Perhaps we can build there again, when things get back to normal. Goodbye for now."

"Goodbye," said Mother. She put her arm around me and we waved until Mrs King and the boys disappeared around the corner. As we turned to go to the house, a voice called out of the darkness.

"Mum, Katie, stop."

We turned around again and saw a woman running toward us. For a moment we stood, not believing our eyes, then I rushed forward, and threw myself into Helen's arms. Mother was close behind me and the three of us did a little dance in the middle of the road. The few remaining dancers stopped momentarily to watch us, then went back to jitterbugging.

It was several minutes before we were ready to let go of one another.

"Why didn't you let us know you were coming?" mother asked. "You missed the party."

While Helen was explaining to mother that she hadn't had time to let her know, I noticed a man in uniform, standing watching us. I tugged at Helen's arm.

"There's someone watching us," I whispered.

"Oh, yes." She turned round and ran to the man. She spoke to him and taking his hand she led him toward mother and me.

"Mum, Katie, I want you to meet Joe Birch. Joe and I are engaged." She showed us her left hand with a ring on the third finger.

For a moment, there was absolute silence. I looked at Mother. Her mouth was open but no sound was coming out.

At last she closed her mouth and held out her hand to this stranger.

"Forgive me, Mr Birch," she stammered. "How do you do?"

"There's nothing to forgive, Mrs Wells. You've had a shock. Please call me Joe."

"Well yes, you could say I have had a shock. I'm sure I will like you when I have had a chance to get to know you. Say hello to Joe, Katie."

"Hello Joe," I said. I was not sure if I liked him or not. I had just got Helen back and now it seemed I was going to lose her again.

"I'm sorry to have given you a shock, Mum. These things just happen. Blame the war."

"Well, let's get inside where we can talk without half the neighbourhood listening. Come along Katie, it's time you were in bed."

Inside the house mother said, "Take Joe into the living room, Helen." Turning to me, she said, "And you, come with me and help me make the tea. You may stay up a little longer."

While mother boiled the water for tea, I put the few biscuits I found in the biscuit tin onto a small plate and put it and four cups and saucers on a tray. Mother said, "Take that into the living room and bring the empty tray back, so I can put the teapot and sugar and milk on it."

I did as I was told and after a few minutes, we were all sipping our tea and nibbling on biscuits. I was about to reach for a second one when mother caught my eye and slowly shaking her head looked toward Helen and Joe.

"How did you two meet?" Mother asked.

"Do you remember what I told you about losing my ball of wool in the train, and a man pulling it back into the carriage?"

Mother and I looked at one another and grinned. "Yes," we said in unison.

Helen laughed. "Well that gentleman was Joe. I didn't know him at the time, but about six months ago, I went to the canteen to get some lunch. I had my knitting with me to do while I ate, and I had it on the tray. As I walked to a table, the ball of wool fell off the tray. I bent down to pick it up, but another hand reached it first. A voice said, 'Do you make a habit of catching innocent young men with your wool?' The voice sounded familiar and when I looked up, I realised who had spoken."

"She looked as surprised as you did Mrs Wells, when Helen told you we were engaged," Joe said, laughing.

"Yes, I was surprised. I had hoped I would never see any of the people from that humiliating night again, ever," Helen said poking Joe playfully in the ribs.

He grasped the tickling hand and kissed it. "She was enough of a lady not to tell me that at the time, and instead asked if I would like to have lunch with her. She even offered to pay for it as a reward for saving her wool. Of course I rejected the offer of payment, and when I had bought my meal, I joined her to eat it. We exchanged names and spent a happy hour filling in each other on where we had been, and what we had been doing for the last four years."

"And where had you been?" Mother asked.

"Before the dreaded wool incident, I was in France, where I was wounded in the leg. That night, I was on leave recuperating from surgery. When I recovered, I was sent to Italy and in November last year, I got in the way of an Italian sniper. The army decided I should come back to England, to save on future medical bills. When I was fit for duty again, I was sent up north to the camp Helen was in. When Helen and I met in the canteen, I had just arrived."

"I told Joe about you and Katie, Mum, and about Dad fighting his second World War and Joe told me about his family. When our officers told us we could have forty-eight hours leave at the same time, we decided to visit our families. We went to Joe's home this morning, and we will spend tomorrow with you and Katie if that's okay with you."

"Of course it's okay," said mother. "I can make up the bed for Joe in your room Helen, if you are willing to share Katie's bed."

"Oh, Helen, say you will. I've missed you so much," I cried.

Helen and Joe looked at one another and then at mother.

"That'll be fine. Thank you, Mrs Wells," Joe said.

"Yes, thanks Mum," said Helen.

I ran across the room and hugged them both. I decided that I liked Joe.

While mother and Helen made up the bed in Helen's bedroom, I got into my pyjamas and then brushed my teeth. I got into bed and lay down, leaving the larger space for Helen. Mother came in and kissed me goodnight, and I heard Helen going downstairs again. I wanted to stay awake until she came to bed, but the party and the excitement of seeing Jimmy and Dougie, and then Helen and Joe, was too much for my body. The next thing I knew it was morning, and I was alone in my bed once more.

Helen was already up and I was disappointed that we had not had time together to talk about Joe and the wedding to come. I reminded myself that Helen was going to stay with us today, and soon she would be leaving the army forever. Then we would be able to see one another whenever we wanted to, and not when some officer said we could.

When I went downstairs, Mother, Helen, and Joe were already eating some of the eggs the hens had laid since we had hardboiled the eggs for sandwiches. I was soon tucking into a mound of scrambled eggs and toast.

When I had finished eating, Mother said, "Don't forget to feed the chickens Katie. I've put the potato peelings in the dish."

"May I help you?" Joe asked.

"Yes please. I'm very proud of my chickens."

I put on my pinafore and picked up the dish of peelings. We left mother and Helen washing and wiping the dishes. I showed Joe where the grain was kept in the wash-house, and let him mix it into the peelings. Then we put the food into three dishes and took them to the henhouses, where the hens clustered noisily around the doors when they saw us coming. I opened the doors and shooed them back so that Joe could put the dishes in the runs.

While the chickens ate, I checked the nest boxes and found six still-warm eggs. I showed them to Joe and then put them into my pinafore pocket.

"I take my hat off to you," said Joe. "I reckon that by providing eggs for your neighbours, you've done as much to help win this war as I have fighting. I bet keeping chickens is hard work. Well done, Katie Wells."

I felt myself blushing. "Thank you Joe." I am sure that when we walked back to the house I was several inches taller.

As we entered the kitchen, I heard Helen saying to Mother, "I thought we could use my ration coupons to buy some goodies and have a picnic in the park today."

"Oh I am glad you have some coupons, Helen. I was wondering what I could give you for lunch. A picnic sounds wonderful."

"Sure does," said Joe. Take Katie with you and I'll keep your mother company."

"Okay Katie, you come with me. You can show me the best shops to go to."

Our first shop was the grocer's. Helen showed the grocer what coupons she had, and they discussed the best things to get for them. We came out with a small slab of butter, some cheese, and a tin of Spam.

"Let's try the baker now, Katie."

Bread was not rationed yet, so Helen was able to buy a crusty loaf and four sticky buns. Mother always complained that the bakers supplemented the flour with sawdust because the white bread was grey.

At the house, we found Joe pulling a lettuce from the garden and weeding between mother's rows of vegetables.

"Be careful," warned Helen. "You may find yourself taken prisoner by Mum if you make yourself too useful."

Joe laughed. "Don't tempt me. I would give myself up in a heartbeat. Your Mum's quite the gardener."

"Okay. Carry on soldier. Katie take the shopping in to Mum and tell her I'll be in in a minute."

I knew when I was not wanted, so I reluctantly left. Before going into the house, I looked back to where Joe was trying to steal a kiss, and Helen was giggling and protesting that his hands were covered in dirt. I decided that Helen was not the only member of the family who loved Joe. I hoped that I would have a boyfriend, one day. I remembered Arthur Merriweather and how I had wanted a boyfriend as handsome as he was. Poor Jenny and Joy. *Please God, find someone to love and take care of them,* I prayed.

Mother made thick-sliced sandwiches of Spam and cheese, split the buns and filled them with jam, and wrapped everything in a tea towel. She made tea in the thermos and put everything in her shopping basket, along with four mugs and a tablecloth.

Joe carried the basket and we set out for the park. What a treat it was to go out without worrying about the possibility of seeing a V-1 chugging into sight, or a V-2 streaking from the sky.

Joe and Mother pushed me and Helen on the swings, and Joe ran round and round pushing the roundabout, to make it go faster. When I moved to the slide, he and Helen joined me. Helen reached the ground safely, but Joe got stuck and had to be pushed and pulled to the bottom. We played hide and seek and threw a tennis ball around until the adults sank to the ground breathing hard and claiming exhaustion.

At last, Helen looked at her watch and said, "I'm afraid Joe and I will have to leave now. We'll go back to the house with you and Katie, Mum, to pick up our bags. We'll go to the station from there. You can come with us to see us off, if you like, or we can say our goodbyes at the house."

"I don't want you to go. Can't you stay now the war's over?" I pleaded.

"Sorry love. No, we can't stay today. Maybe the next time I come home."

The house felt very empty when we returned after seeing Helen and Joe off, on the train. *Maybe the next time,* I kept saying to myself. Maybe the next time. Please let the next time come soon.

Chapter 18

In the next weeks, the euphoria created by the ending of the war in Europe was tempered by the news coming out of Germany. The advancing Allied Armies found the concentration camps, where anyone who did not fit the Fuhrer's idea of what a human is, had been incarcerated. Pictures on the cinema newsreels showed us twisted, naked, entwined bodies of men women and children in mass graves, and living skeletons clutching the wire fences around their prisons.

The instigator of this horror had died by his own hand, but this could not erase the memory of what had been done in his name. His subordinates eventually came to trial and were executed or imprisoned, adding to the carnage created by this madman, Hitler.

What madness is in mankind that we conceive of such atrocities? Where was God while this was happening? To my child's mind, things were black and white, right or wrong. I could see no reason for God to let so many innocent men, women, and children suffer as they had done. I had been told that God loved us. The concentration camps created the third chink in my belief in a loving God; the first being when Jimmy's grandmother had died; the second when Joy's father was killed.

Now that the war in Europe was over, Father and Helen could write to us without the censor wielding his black pencil on their letters home. Two days after Helen went back to camp, she wrote to tell us how impressed Joe was by mother and me. She also hinted that if father came home soon, the wedding might happen before her demob from the army. Demobilisation depended on the age of the person and how long they had served, so Helen might have to wait a while to get out of the army. However, if she was married, she would be demobilised immediately.

Mother had written to tell Father about Helen and Joe, and two weeks later, a letter came from him. He said that he looked forward to meeting Joe so that he could determine whether or not he was good enough for his elder daughter. This worried me. I liked Joe and the thought that father would not let him marry Helen upset me. When I told Mother this, she said Father was only joking. This made me feel better but I wished I could have seen father when he said it. "He should have written, 'ha, ha' ha,' after he wrote that, then I would have known he was joking," I grumbled.

Mother laughed. "You tell him that when he comes home. Let's see what else he has to say." She went back to reading:

> *"My ship is coming home. We should reach Portsmouth sometime in the next week or two and I think I will be demobbed quite soon after that. I hope the wedding will wait for me to come home. I want to walk my daughter down the aisle."*

"There you are, Katie. I told you, Daddy was joking."

> *"I hope you and Katie are well. It is such a relief to know that you are safe. I can't wait to see you again. Take care, my lovelies.*
>
> *Hugs and kisses. See you soon.*
>
> *Love,*
>
> *Bill."*

"Oh what wonderful news Katie. I must write to Helen and tell her about Daddy coming home. She'll be so pleased."

For the next two weeks, mother and I ate our breakfast every day with one ear on the radio, and one on the front door. As soon as we heard the click of the letterbox, we raced to the hall to pick up the mail from the doormat. I was not home when the second mail of the day came, but when the letter from Father arrived, Mother kept it until I got home from school in the afternoon. She had been watching for me to come down the street. As soon as she saw me, she rushed out of the house to meet me, waving the envelope in her hand.

"Katie, Katie, Daddy's letter has come."

I ran to meet her and mother tore open the letter and began to read.

> *"Dear Beth and Katie,*
>
> *Get out the WELCOME HOME banner. My ship docked in Portsmouth this morning and the crew is going on leave two days from today. I can't wait to be with you. Must stop and get this in the post.*
>
> *See you soon.*
>
> *Love,*
>
> *Bill"*

Mother looked at the date on the letter. "My goodness, Daddy will be here tomorrow. We'd better get the house shipshape and Bristol fashion."

I had no idea what Bristol fashion was but I was happy to be doing whatever mother wanted. I hadn't seen father since that night before the Christmas when I showed him my new shoes. I had long outgrown them. Would Father recognize me?

We had a quick tea and started vacuuming, dusting, polishing, scrubbing, and putting away anything that was not where it should be. The window boards had been leaning against the wall in the sitting room since the night raids had ended. Mother looked at them.

"What shall we do with these, Katie?"

"Why don't we put them in the air raid shelter?" I suggested.

"Good thinking, Sherlock. We'll carry them between us, two at a time."

It took several trips but we finally dropped the last two boards into the shelter. We were both sore, with aching legs and stiff backs.

"Thank you, Katie. Without your help, I'd have still been carrying boards when the moon rose."

"What will Daddy do with the shelter?" I asked.

"I don't know, but I expect he will think of something. I can't see him digging it up."

She put her arm around my shoulders to walk back to the house and I realised just how much I had grown. The last time father saw me, I had been small enough to hold his hand in the street and cuddle up on his knee. Somehow I could not see me doing that now.

"Mummy, do you think that Daddy will recognize me?"

Mother gave me a quizzical look. "Of course he will. He'll be surprised at how you've grown, but he'll know who you are. Wait 'til he sees you in your school uniform. He'll be so proud of you."

She gave me a big hug and I was reassured. Probably father had changed too, but I was sure I would remember him.

Father had not said what time he would be home, but the next day, mother said I could take the day off school so that I could be sure to be home when he did arrive. We were both jittery with excitement. Mother worried about what meals to prepare. Should she make lunch for two or three, and should we eat at the usual time, or wait, in case father arrived just after we finished. What could she make for supper? She had not had time to make sure we had enough food, by saving coupons.

"Make an omelette," I suggested. "You can make chips with the potatoes from last winter. We have lettuce in the garden, and there may be a few small ripe tomatoes in the greenhouse to make a salad."

"Great. I am so excited I can't think straight. I picked up ten eggs when I fed the chickens this morning. Oh dear. I wonder how Daddy will feel about the smell of boiled potato peel."

"He'll love it when you give him the omelette," I assured her.

"Thanks Katie. I don't know why I am so nervous."

I thought I knew. If I was worried that father would not recognize me, how must mother feel about this meeting after such a long time. The war had not treated her kindly. There were a few grey hairs among the dark brown ones and the strain of worrying about Father, Helen, and me had created some lines on her face. Perhaps Father would have changed too. We had no idea what the war had done to him.

We did wait lunch until we were too hungry to wait any longer, and mother made us sandwiches and the always-welcome cups of tea. After lunch, I suggested that we weed the vegetable rows in the front garden to fill the time, and from there we would see father coming when he did arrive. We set to, thinning the rows of carrots, and idly chatting as we worked. It was very hot and I was soon sweating and thirsty.

"Would you like me to get us some water to drink, Mummy?" I asked.

"That would be nice. Thanks Katie."

I stood up and was surprised to see a heavily bearded man looking over the garden gate. "Nice little garden you have there," he said.

At the sound of the voice, Mother leapt to her feet and rushed toward the man.

"Bill, oh Bill."

I gazed in amazement as Mother and this man, whom I realized must be Father, hugged and kissed over the gate. At last they broke their hold on one another and father said, "Let's get this gate open before it's permanently embossed on my stomach."

Mother moved back and opened the gate. Father stepped into the garden and gathered me to him in a big bear hug. Then he stood back and looked at me. "My, you've grown Katie, but I would have known you anywhere." Tears sprang into his eyes and he wiped them away with his hand. "I have missed so much of your childhood. I'm sorry."

Now I was crying. "That's all right," I said. "I am sorry I didn't know who you were."

Father chuckled. "How could you know me when all you could see of me were my eyes. Your mother has listened to my voice a lot longer than you have. She might have wondered who I was, if I hadn't spoken. When I get in the house, I'll bathe and shave this beard off, and then I'll be your daddy again. We have a lot to catch up on, you and I."

He turned back to Mother and took her hand before picking up his kit bag. "Come on. The carrots will need a rest after you two have worked on them, and I could use a cup of tea."

Oh that ubiquitous cup of tea. No matter what happens; whether the situation is dire or happy, a "cuppa tea" always fits the bill. To the English it is the cure-all for all ills.

While Mother boiled the water, Father took his bath and shaved all the hair from his face. When he came into the kitchen, I could see the man I remembered, despite the added lines, which had developed, partly from the passage of time and partly from gazing into the limitless horizon of the ocean.

He put his arms around Mother's waist as she laid out cups and saucers for the tea.

"Do you want something to eat?" Mother asked him. "I only have bread and jam and a little cheese I'm afraid. I didn't have time to stockpile coupons for your arrival. You didn't say how long you can stay. When Helen comes, she usually brings food coupons, if she is here for more than a day."

"I'm sorry, I didn't know how long a leave I would have until this morning. I am here for three days and yes I have food coupons. I also managed to persuade the cook to give me a few tins of food and packets of biscuits to bring home. I'll get them."

"No sit down and have your tea unless you want some of the biscuits to eat."

"I'm sure Katie wouldn't say no to a biscuit, would you Katie?"

My tongue tried to say it didn't matter but my eyes gave me away. Father got up and brought his kitbag to the kitchen. After some scrabbling about in the bag, he came up with a packet of digestive biscuits. Mother put them on a plate and we all enjoyed the unexpected treat.

Tea drunk and biscuits munched we sat, not quite knowing what to say. A large chunk of mine and Mother's lives was unknown to father and the same period of his life was unknown to us. Mother and father held hands and looked longingly into one another's eyes. I felt like a piece of luggage not wanted on the journey.

After a few uncomfortable minutes, I stood up and collected the cups, saucers, and plates. "I'll wash these and put them away. Why don't you and Daddy..." There was silence while I searched for what I could suggest they might do. Eventually, I came out with, "...have a rest."

Mother and Father grinned at one another. "Thank you Katie. That is very kind of you. We will go upstairs for a little while," said father. "We have a lot to, um, talk about."

I heard them giggling like two-year-olds as they climbed the stairs and I turned the sink tap on full blast, to cover any noises coming from the bedroom.

Father's three-day leave flew by, but saying goodbye this time was tempered by the knowledge that it would be the last time we would have to do it. On his return to his ship, his captain informed him that his demobilization papers had come, and that once he had reported to the office to sign off and been supplied with civilian clothes, he was free to go home.

The next day he said goodbye to his shipmates, was thanked for his service to his country, given some medals and a suit to wear in exchange for his uniform, and released from his duties. By teatime, he was home again, much to my surprise when I came home from school.

The next day, Father went to see the manager of the bank where he had worked before the war, and was told that his job was still his when he was ready to return. He took a week at home before returning, and little by little, we came to know one another again.

He mended the cracks in the pond and covered the whole base with coats of cement. It took several hours to fill the pond with water. On Saturday morning, we all went to the plant nurseries, searching for water lily plants and to pet shops for goldfish. One of the nurseries suggested that we find a public pond, which had some water lilies in it and take a cutting. Father said we would have to think about that. We struck lucky at the third pet shop we visited. The owner was a fish fancier and he sold us half a dozen small fish from his own aquarium and fish food from his stock.

There were a few puppies in the second pet shop, and I reminded mother of her promise to buy a dog after the war. She reminded me that meat was still rationed and that perhaps we should wait a little while. We had Bob to think of too. He might not want a dog in the house. Reluctantly, I said goodbye to the puppies, and determined not to let Mother forget her promise.

Helen wrote to say that she would like to bring Joe home to meet father at the next weekend, and discuss a date for the wedding. They would only be with us for the Sunday.

I was very happy that Helen and Joe were coming, but a little worried about what father would think of Joe. I really did not know father well enough to guess what kind of man he wanted for Helen, and he seemed to take his duty as a father very seriously. I told him how much I liked Joe, and what he had said about my raising chickens, to the point that father said, "Are you sure it's not you who wants to marry Joe?"

I decided I had better say no more on the subject.

When Sunday came, I waited eagerly for Helen and Joe to arrive. I was helping father weed the vegetable beds in the back garden, when I heard the latch on the front gate click. I leapt up and started to run to the house. Father followed and went to wash the dirt off his hands before hugging Helen and shaking Joe's hand. I anxiously watched, trying to gauge father's opinion of Joe. At least he was being polite, which I felt was a good sign. We all went into the sitting room, until mother asked me to lay the table for lunch while she dished up the food.

I tried to hear what was happening in the sitting room, but I could only hear an occasional word in a mumble of conversation. I heard mother go and tell them dinner was served and they all came into the dining room; father with mother, and Helen and Joe holding hands.

Mother had used coupons from all three ration books to buy a small roast and had made Yorkshire pudding, cooked around the meat. Joe said it was a veritable feast, and that he hoped Helen could cook as well as her mother. "You could teach the camp cook a few things Mrs Wells," he said, smiling at her.

"I second that," said Father. "Some of the meals the ship's cook produced would make your hair curl. One day he made Spotted Dick for dessert and cooked it in someone's sock. Several helpings had parts of the owner's numbers on them."

Joe looked as though he didn't know how to react to what father had said.

"Oh Bill, don't tease," said mother. "What will Joe think of you?"

"Me teasing?" Father put on his much-maligned look. "Would I tease you about something as important as Spotted Dick? The captain complained that his piece was too small to even get a number."

By now we were all laughing and Joe relaxed.

Dessert for us was apples, bottled the previous autumn, served with custard.

"Thank you, Mrs Wells. That was delicious," said Joe. "Can I help with the dishes?"

"No you can't, Joe. None of you left anything on your plates to be cleaned off. They won't take a minute to wash and dry. Helen and Katie will help me. You and Helen's dad go into the sitting room, and we'll join you for a cup of tea when we finish in the kitchen."

"Yes, Joe. Let's you and me go and let our dinner settle while we talk business."

Joe kissed Helen on the cheek and followed father to the sitting room.

"What business are they talking about?" I enquired anxiously.

"Men's business. Nothing for you to worry about," said mother. "Come on, let's get this stuff cleared away while we talk women's business."

The women's business was about when and where the wedding would be. Helen wanted a Church wedding, which meant talking to the minister and getting the banns read.

"That means it can't be until July," said Mother. She suggested that Helen and Joe should go to see the minister that afternoon. She and Helen pored over the calendar, fixing on a suitable date, and discussed whom to invite to the wedding breakfast. That was difficult, with the rationing still in effect. The wedding breakfast would have to be minimal, unless we had fish and chips, which were almost the only food not rationed. There were rumours that snook, a fish previously unknown to the English, which sometimes appeared on the boards in the fish shop, was whale; neither of which held much appeal for the British palate. Then there was leave to be arranged with the army for both Helen and Joe.

By the time all that had been dealt with, the tea was steeped and ready to be poured. Mother knocked on the sitting room door, which struck me as odd at the time, but it was quickly opened by father. Joe stood as we entered, took the tray from mother, and placed it on the table. We sat down and Mother poured the tea.

"Have you got the wedding date fixed?" Father asked Helen.

I said a little thank you under my breath. Whatever the men's business was, apparently it had gone well and Father approved of Joe.

Helen told Joe and Father what she and Mother had decided, and asked Joe if that was okay with him.

"Of course, if we can both get leave," he said. "I'll get to work on it as soon as we get back to camp."

"Mum thought we should go to see the minister this afternoon, because it will take three weeks to read the banns."

"Okay, we'll go as soon as we've drunk our tea."

I waved goodbye to Helen and Joe, and waited anxiously for their return. Father suggested that I help him weed the vegetables in the back garden, to pass the time, but I remembered what had happened when Mother and I were waiting for Father, and I wanted to see Helen and Joe as soon as they turned into the road. So I stayed in the house and watched from the front window. At last they came around the corner and I rushed up the road to meet them.

"When will the wedding be?" I called out.

"Get the town crier to announce it, why don't you?" said Helen, ruffling my hair. "The wedding will be the twenty-eighth of July."

I clapped my hands. "Good, that's the first day of the school summer holiday."

"I'm glad it fits into your timetable," said Joe. "We would have had to change it, if you couldn't be there."

"Don't be silly, Joe. I don't go to school on a Saturday."

By now, we were back at the house and I ran in to tell mother when the wedding would be. Then I ran to the chicken house to tell Clucky the good news.

Helen and Joe had to return to the camp that evening, so after supper, we walked with them to the station to say our goodbyes.

"Let me know when the leaves are approved," said nother, "and I'll get started on arranging the printing of the invitations."

"Will do. I'll be waiting outside the officer's room when he gets back from breakfast tomorrow morning."

We waved them off as the train left the station and walked home with joy in our steps.

"We are going to be very busy for the next few weeks," said mother to me. "You'll have to help me write the invitations and make the wedding cake. I hope I have the right-sized cake pans. I doubt I'll find any in the stores."

Mother mumbled to herself all the way home. Father winked at me. He bent down and whispered in my ear. "All we are going to hear about from now on is the wedding. Learn how to turn a deaf ear is my advice."

Chapter 19

Father was right. Mother talked wedding every opportunity she got. Of course, the neighbours had to be told. After school the next day, Vicky came running over to see me. "Mum told me about the wedding," she cried. "Will you be a bridesmaid?"

This surprised me. It had never occurred to me that I would not be a bridesmaid. "I expect so, but nothing has been said about it. I hope I will."

"Oh I'm sure you will. You'll have to be. Who else could Helen have?"

I shrugged. "I don't know. Perhaps a friend," I suggested.

"Well it might be better if you weren't a bridesmaid again."

"Why?"

"Well you have already been a bridesmaid, haven't you?"

"Yes. What's that got to do with anything?"

"Well my mum says, 'Three times a bridesmaid, never a bride.' I'll want you to be my bridesmaid, and that will make three times. That will mean you'll never be a bride."

I frowned. "That's silly. I've never heard of that. How can the number of times I am a bridesmaid mean I won't be a bride?"

Vicky shrugged. "I dunno. It's just something people say. Probably isn't true. Forget I said it."

But I couldn't forget it. I had taken it for granted that I would be Helen's bridesmaid, but what if Helen did want to have a friend as a bridesmaid? The only wedding I had been to was Jenny's and that had been a very quiet affair at the Registry Office. Perhaps a church wedding was different and only adults took part. Now Vicky had created another problem. I would have liked to be Vicky's bridesmaid when she got married, but if that was going to mean that I would not be able to marry, I would have to not be her bridesmaid. This wedding was beginning to be a Pandora's box. I felt as though something sinister might be raining on my parade. I decided to ask Mother about it.

When she came to kiss me goodnight that evening, I asked her if she thought I would be Helen's bridesmaid.

"Yes, of course you will. Whatever made you think you wouldn't?"

"Perhaps Helen would like to have a friend as her bridesmaid."

"Well, she can have a friend, or more if she wants, but you must be one of them. You are her sister and you know you mean the world to her. The real question is, what are you going to wear? For that matter what is Helen going to wear? Clothes are still rationed. Perhaps we can ask Jenny and Auntie Em if they can spare some coupons for us. We can use ours and Daddy's. He can wear his new demob suit. I can wear one of my old pre-war party dresses that I haven't had a chance to wear since the war began. I'll get to work on the clothes coupons tomorrow."

I could see she was off in wedding land again. She made to get off the bed and leave. "Don't go, Mum. I need to ask you something else." I told her what Vicky had said about being a bridesmaid three times.

"Oh that's an old wives' tale. You don't need to worry about that. I was a bridesmaid four times before marrying your father." With that she left the room, muttering names of possible people she could call on for donations of clothes coupons. I began to think that I would elope to Gretna Green when I married. I didn't think Mother would be able to go through another wedding and remain sane. I would have to talk to Father about using the ladder he used to paint the outside of the house. For now, I could stop worrying about whether or not I would be a bridesmaid for three times and simply think of what to wear at Helen's wedding. I would discuss it with Helen when she came home on leave.

A week went by before a letter came from Helen. Everything was arranged. She had been given two-weeks leave starting on the twenty-third of July, after which she would receive her demobilization papers on her return to camp on the fifth of August. Joe had been given two-weeks leave starting on the twenty-fifth July and ending on August seventh. Joe had made arrangements for them to go away after the wedding, but he refused to tell Helen where they were going. Helen was also coming home for two days; Friday and Saturday, in a week's time.

Mother wrote back telling Helen that she was collecting clothing coupons from neighbours and friends. She was going to use some for a bridesmaid's dress for me, and the rest would be used for Helen. She also asked if Helen needed coupons for other bridesmaids.

It seemed that I was going to be a bridesmaid whether Helen wanted me or not. However, I decided that I would tell Helen that she didn't have to have me if she didn't want to. I wanted to be reassured that Helen loved me. I was spared having to ask Helen anything. She wrote back quickly to say that I was the only one she wanted as her bridesmaid, and she hoped that I was happy to take on that important role. How could I ever have doubted her?

Helen arrived home the next week, late on Thursday evening.

Mother told her what she had been doing in the way of wedding preparations.

"Aunt Em and Jenny have given us some clothing coupons, and Mrs Cooper, next door, and Mrs Davis, and all Katie's egg customers have contributed. I have got the invitations from the printer, and I am saving sugar and dried fruit for the cake. Katie wondered if you wanted to have another bridesmaid, and I wondered if you had considered asking Jenny to be a bridesmaid?"

"No, Mum I hadn't, because of the problems with the clothing rations, but if she and Aunt Em can use the coupons they've given to me, that would be ideal. Jenny has already been married and has a child so she will be my Matron of Honour." A frown wrinkled Helen's forehead. "I wonder though, Mum. You don't think she might be upset do you? After what happened to her? A wedding might make her remember her own wedding and Arthur. It could be distressing for her. How is Jenny?"

"Oh, Helen, that hadn't entered my head. I suppose it might bring back memories she'd rather forget. Jenny seems okay. She has a job and Joy is in a nursery while she is at work. Katie and I babysit Joy if Jenny and her mum want to go out. Joy is a beautiful child and has brought Jenny solace. I hope that someday Jenny will find another man to love who loves her. She deserves a good husband and Joy should have a father." Mother sighed. "Unhappily, the war has left a lot of young widows and fatherless children. I'll get Aunt Em alone and ask what she thinks."

"Thanks Mum. I'd love to have Jenny in the bridal party, but I would hate to do anything to hurt her."

Helen suggested we go shopping the next day for dresses, and maybe shoes, and find out what we could buy with the coupons.

"Good idea," said mother. "With that in mind, I suggest we get to bed so we can make an early start in the morning. We have got permission for Katie to have the day off school because you are home, Helen."

"Good. Okay, kiddo, let's climb the apples and pears and put our heads on the weeping willow," said Helen putting her arm around me. Father had been born within the sound of Bow Bells, which meant he was a Cockney. Cockneys lived in the East End of London and had devised a rhyming language of their own. Apples and pears were stairs, the weeping willow was a pillow, trouble and strife were a wife. There were many more but father didn't use them except in fun.

Helen and Mum came to kiss me goodnight and reminded me that I had to be up early. This did not help me get to sleep and I lay for some time, thinking about what we were going to do and how much fun it would be. For as long as I could remember, I had only had a new dress, to replace one I had grown out of. I hoped the shops had some really pretty dresses I could choose from. On that thought, I eventually fell asleep.

We were waiting at the doors of the department store as they opened the next morning. I loved going to this store. The counters had seats for the customers to sit on while they made their purchases. It also had an overhead cable system with small cylindrical canisters hanging from it, to carry the money from customers to a cashier in the centre of the store. When I was younger, I harboured ambitions of becoming a sales clerk in this store, so that I could send the canister along the wire. I never tired of watching them bobbing along from every counter, like miniature trams in the sky.

"Let's look at patterns and material first," said Helen.

The pattern books were on a slanted shelf and we found two that had wedding clothes for brides and bridesmaids. I took one, and Helen and mother the other. I turned the pages of dresses with awe. I had never seen such pretty dresses. I could hear mother and Helen talking and working out how many coupons they would need. "That's nice," and "We haven't got enough coupons for that much material," infected my own searching.

When I reached the last page, I turned back to the beginning and found two of the patterns I liked. I put my fingers in the pages to show them to mother when she and Helen had finished looking. At last Helen closed her book and said to me, "Let's change books now Katie."

"I found two that I like in this one," I said.

"Let's see them," said Mother.

I opened the book to the first finger and showed them a dress with layers of frills and bows.

"Hmm," said Mother. "Let's see the next one."

I opened to the second finger. This dress was plainer with a round neckline and a sash, tied into a bow at the back, above a full skirt.

"Yes, I think we may be able to use that one. Let's make a note of the page number and the amount of cloth we need."

That done, we exchanged books. The patterns were much the same as the ones I had already seen and I quickly closed my book, not finding anything I liked better than the two I had already chosen. Helen and mother made notes of a couple more dresses, and we went to look at material. Helen had found six dresses she liked and it took a while for her and mother to work out which ones fit our coupons and our purses.

"We have to save some coupons for shoes," mother reminded us. "What colour material do you want for the bridesmaid and maybe the Matron of Honour?"

"Oh, I think we should let Katie choose the colour."

They both looked at me. I hadn't given colour a thought. I didn't really have a favourite colour. I thought about the flowers we used to have in the garden and I remembered how beautiful it looked in the spring when a great carpet of yellow daffodils covered the black soil.

"Yellow," I said.

Helen smiled. "That will be lovely with your dark hair, Katie."

Mother suggested that I find something that I would be able to wear after the wedding, so while mother and Helen looked at the white cloth, which I thought very plain and unexciting I went to find some yellow cloth. There were bolts of yellow cotton, but they were all patterned with other colours. Then I found a bolt of that white cloth I thought unexciting, and lo and behold, it was covered in tiny sprays of daffodils. I called out to mother and ran to where she and Helen were looking at soft, satiny materials. "Mum, Helen, come and see what I found." I grabbed their hands and pulled them to where the white and yellow cloth lay.

"That's very pretty," said Helen. "Do you think we can get that, Mum?"

Mother looked at the price and the amount of cloth we needed for the second dress. I held my breath and clutched Helen's hand.

"Yes, if we go with the one without the frills, we can manage that and it will be good for everyday or parties. Yes we can."

I hugged mother and did a little jig of enjoyment.

145

"Now let's go and choose your material, Helen," I said.

"I know which material I want. Let's go to the sales clerk and get her to measure it out for us."

We picked up the patterns we wanted and took them to the sales clerk. Mother pointed out the materials, and I watched, fascinated, as the clerk hefted the large rolls of material onto a long table, where a yardstick was sunk into the wooden edge. With many thumps of the roll, she efficiently measured Helen's cloth one yard at a time, folding it against itself as she pulled it out. She wrapped it in tissue paper and brown paper, and then turned to my cloth.

"And this is for the bridesmaid, is it?" she said, smiling down at me as she pulled the second roll to the yard stick. I nodded shyly. "You will look lovely in it. Is the bride your sister?" I nodded again. The clerk smiled at Helen and turned back to me. "She will be a lovely bride won't she?"

"Thank you," said Helen. "For both of us. I think my sister is a bit overcome by it all."

"Oh yes, thank you, she will," I stammered.

The clerk wrapped my cloth up and took it and the patterns to the counter, where she made up the bill and collected the clothing coupons.

I climbed onto one of the chairs and watched her put the bill, coupons, and money into the canister to be carried to the cashier. Off it went, humming along the line, returning a few minutes later. The clerk took the canister down, unscrewed the lid, took out the receipt, and gave some change to mother. We all thanked her and she said, "Thank you. And to the bride, I wish every happiness. May you and your husband enjoy many peaceful years together."

She handed the two parcels and patterns to Helen who said, "Thank you very much. I'm sure we will."

We came out of the store into bright sunshine. Mother looked at her watch.

"It's eleven o'clock. I suggest we go to see Miss Thomas and ask if she will make the dresses. If she can, we won't have to carry these parcels around while we shop."

We were soon ringing Miss Thomas' doorbell, hoping she was home. I breathed a sigh of relief when I heard footsteps coming toward the door.

"Hello, Mrs Wells," said Miss Thomas when she opened the door. "I hope you are bringing me some work?"

"We are, if you have time to make a wedding dress and a brides-maid dress," said Mother.

Miss Thomas stepped back into the hallway. "Come in, come in. How wonderful to be sewing for a young bride. So many of them are in such a hurry these days, they just go off to the registry office."

Miss Thomas was what mother called a 'maiden lady.' She had been engaged to marry a young soldier, who was killed in the trenches of the First World War. Her father had returned from the same trenches, with lungs damaged by poison gas and had lived only a few years after being sent home. Miss Thomas and her mother had nursed him in his last years, and now they lived together in the house where Miss Thomas had been born. Her mother was elderly and frail, and Miss Thomas now looked after her. Her only income came from her sewing. Had I known these things when I was a child, I might have thought more kindly of her. Instead, I thought she was a dried-up, old thing, always wearing black and with her thin-looking, grey hair pulled into a tight bun at the back of her head. Some of the children at school were afraid of her, thinking she was a witch.

Mother, Helen, and I followed Miss Thomas to the back of the house, into a room, which had been turned into a workroom. A cotton-covered body shape on a stand stood in one corner, a rack of small shelves hanging from the wall held cotton reels of every colour I could imagine, and a large table in the centre of the room had a length of cloth, covered in paper pattern pieces pinned upon it. A large window looked out onto the garden, and beneath it stood a treadle sewing machine in its own cabinet. Bits of thread were spread haphazardly over the floor.

"Let me see the patterns," said Miss Thomas and Helen handed them to her. "Very nice and practical too. You could dye this wedding dress and wear it to a dance or dinner party and you," Miss Thomas peered over her wire-framed spectacles at me, "I bet you'll wear this out before you outgrow it."

I was not sure if she considered this a good thing, or was accusing me of not taking care of my clothes.

She pulled a tape measure from around her neck and began to measure Helen.

"Will you be wearing high heels?" she asked.

"Only about two inches," Helen replied.

Miss Thomas added two inches to the measurement. When she was finished with Helen, it was my turn. She looked at Mother. "This pattern is for a short skirt. Is that what you want? I could make it long if you have enough material."

"I bought a little more than we need, to allow for growth," said Mother. "I don't know if there is enough to make it full length."

"If I can make it long, would you like that?" Miss Thomas asked me.

"Oh, yes please."

"All right. I'll see what I can do. Your mother can always cut it down for you to wear everyday."

Suddenly, my opinion of Miss Thomas was changed. She couldn't be a witch, unless she was a good one. I stood very still while my measurements were taken. Miss Thomas finished writing them on her pad.

"Now when is the wedding and when can you come for a fitting?"

"The twenty-eighth of July and I will be home from the twenty-third of July. Will that be all right for you?"

Miss Thomas looked at her calendar. "Yes that will be fine. I expect Katie can come in any time, can't she?" she asked Mother.

"Yes, outside of school hours. There may be a Matron of Honour. Will you be able to make her dress too?"

"I think so. If I can't, I will ask someone else to help me. That may cost a little more, I'm afraid."

"No problem," said Helen. "Thank you very much, Miss Thomas. I'll let Mum know which day I can come for the fitting, and she can tell you."

There were more thanks and goodbyes and we left Miss Thomas standing at her front door.

Mother looked at her watch and said, "It's time to eat and my feet need a rest. Let's go to the fish shop and buy fish and chips for lunch."

The fish shop was busy, as it always was on Fridays. The smells of hot fat, vinegar, and heat greeted us at the open door. We joined the queue of people waiting to be served. One at a time, they reached the counter where the owner, Mr Jones, took the order and shouted it out to Mrs Jones, who was cooking the food. Their daughter put a piece of white paper onto some sheets of newspaper and stood beside the fryers, while her mother put the fish and chips onto the paper.

"I hope we get served soon. These smells are making me hungry," I complained.

"Make up your mind what you want and then you can go," said Mother. "Because we were going shopping, I forgot to bring any newspaper with me. You can run home, get some old newspaper from the laundry shed, and run back here before we reach the counter. One less person in here will make it cooler too."

I looked at the menu on the wall. There was not much to choose from; Cod and chips, or haddock and chips. "I'll have the cod with chips, please," I said.

"Okay. Off you go. Be quick."

I ran along the street and grabbed the newspaper that Mother had put aside to take to the fishmonger. I was hotter now than I had been in the fish shop, but I ran back as fast as I could. Mother and Helen were still two people from the counter. Some others were standing out of line, obviously waiting for their orders.

"Give the newspapers to Mr Jones," Mother said. "We're waiting for more chips to cook," she explained.

I did as I was told and Mr Jones thanked me. Mrs Jones called out to him. "Chips are ready."

All was bustle again and mother said, "You can go home again Katie, and lay the table for lunch."

I didn't run this time. I was home and had the table laid before mother and Helen arrived.

After lunch, we set out again to look for shoes. This took longer than getting the dress material. The first shop had no white shoes; the second had only one pair for Helen, which she did not like and nothing in children's sizes. Mother suggested that we look for sandals instead of shoes and I found a pair in the next shop. Helen, however, had set her heart on having nice little white pumps and when the last shop in the High Street had nothing, she decided to give up. "I'll see if I can find something near the camp," she sighed.

On the way home, mother said we could go to Aunt Em's house and find out if she was home from work. She was and invited us to have a cup of tea. After trailing round the stores all afternoon, we were glad to sit down.

Mother told Aunt Em why we had come and after a few minutes thinking, Aunt Em said she would ask Jenny if she would like to be Helen's Matron of Honour. "It's hard to know whether it would cheer her up or upset her," she said. "But if she doesn't want to do it, it might be easier for her to refuse through me than to tell you to your face, Helen."

"Yes, I understand. That is why we came to you first, aunt. The last thing I want to do is make her feel she has to do this for me."

"Thank you for thinking of her, Helen. She will appreciate that."

"I would not want anyone else, but please tell her that I will understand if she says no."

"I'll ask her as soon as she comes home.

"We'll give you as many clothing coupons as we can, but I'm afraid you will probably have to use some of your own," mother explained. "Miss Thomas can make a dress for Jenny. Katie's dress is white with tiny daffodils on it, but Jenny can pick whatever material and pattern she wants."

"Okay. I'll let you know tomorrow how she feels," said Aunt Em. "She'll be home soon, so if you don't want to bump into her, you'd better be on your way."

"Right, we'll get out of your way. Thanks for the tea. I needed that. This shopping is exhausting."

"Yes, thanks aunt," said Helen.

I gave aunt a kiss. "'Bye auntie. I hope Jenny will say yes."

"We'll see, Katie. 'Bye now."

Aunt Em called in on her way to work, the next morning. Helen opened the door.

"I'm sorry Helen. Jenny says thank you for wanting her to be your Matron of Honour. She would have loved to be part of your wedding, but she is afraid she might get teary and spoil things."

"Oh aunt. I am sorry but I understand. I hope she will feel able to come to the church. No one will mind if she cries. I bet Dad will cry. They should sit together. I mean it. If Joy was older, I would have her in the wedding party."

That afternoon, Helen left for her camp, armed with all the coupons we had left and determined to find a pair of white pumps with a two-inch heel.

"See you soon," she called as we waved goodbye at the station.

Chapter 20

Mother had been saving food coupons to have the ingredients to make a wedding cake. I came home from school one afternoon, to find her with flour on her face and sleeves pushed up to her elbows. She was mixing flour, sugar, eggs, and dried fruits in a large bowl and mumbling to herself as she worked. Two cake pans; one large and one a little smaller, stood lined with greaseproof paper on the kitchen table.

"Hi Mum. You look busy," I commented.

Mother wiped her streaming face with her sleeve, depositing more flour across her forehead. "Whew it's so hot isn't it? And I haven't turned the oven on yet. I don't know about these cakes. I've never made a wedding cake before. I'm making a Christmas cake, or as near to, given the food restrictions. I'm very glad your hens are all laying. Come and look. Do you think it looks all right?"

I peered into the bowl. My Domestic Science class hadn't dealt with wedding cakes yet. A gorgeous aroma of spices rose from the mixture. "I suppose it's okay, Mum," I ventured. "Are you following the recipe?"

"Sort of, but I keep thinking something is missing."

She began listing things on her fingers. It sounded good to me but what did I know? She stood thinking for a few minutes and then: "I know what's missing. Brandy. I wonder if we have any." She wiped her hands on her apron and hurried to the sitting room. I heard a cupboard being opened and then a cry of triumph. "Hooray."

She came hurrying back, grasping a small bottle in her hand. She took the lid off the bottle and held it upside down over the bowl of cake mixture. I did not see how much brandy was in the bottle, but mother poured until nothing more came out.

"There," she said. "That should do it." I had visions of the wedding guests falling off their chairs after eating their cake.

Mother gave the mixture another stir and said, "Katie, hold the cake pans while I pour the mixture into them."

I wrapped my hands around the largest pan and mother tipped the bowl over it. When it was about three-quarters full she said, "Now the smaller one." The procedure was repeated and mother smoothed out the surface of each cake with her spatula.

"There. I'll let them sit for a bit while the oven warms up. They only need a moderate oven, so they will need a few hours to cook. I have to think about decorating them next."

I shook my head. I would have to warn Dad to expect bouts of hysteria for the next week or so.

That evening, Mother got out the invitations that she had had printed. "Come along you two," she said to father and me. "Come and help me write these." I was tempted to say I had homework to do, but mother knew that school exams were finished. She would never believe that the teachers were giving out homework.

Father put his newspaper down with a sigh, and sat at the dining table. Mother gave each of us a list of names and addresses to put on the invitations and envelopes. There was only the sound of scratching of pen nib on paper, and the smell of cake cooking for the next two hours, as we worked through our lists. The timer rang to tell mother that the cakes were done, and we all put our pens down with relief. All that was needed now was to put the stamps on the envelopes, and mother had not bought those yet.

For the wedding breakfast, father had booked the reception room in The Duck and Drake, the local pub. I thought that was a mistake. We would be eating it at five o'clock in the afternoon. The publican would provide the meal of chicken cacciatore with seasonal vegetables. Mother's cake would end the dinner followed by dancing.

I underestimated Mother when I thought the icing of the cake would be a disaster in progress. The war had denied her the chance to make birthday cakes, and she went to town on the wedding cake. Her royal icing covered the cake like an ice-covered pond. Her decorating tubes were brought out of hibernation and put to work. Under mother's hands, flowers and doves spread across the cakes' surfaces. Helen and Joe's names were written in copperplate lettering on the top of the smaller cake, beneath sugar figurines of a bride and groom. When Mother showed it to me, I gasped.

"Mum. It is beautiful. Where did you learn to do that?"

"Once upon a time, before Helen was born, I decorated cakes for a living. I wasn't sure I could still do it, but I found that I can. When Helen was a child, I made her some lovely birthday cakes. I don't suppose you remember any of the ones I did for you before the war."

"No I don't. I am so sorry, Mum. I don't remember too much about the time before the war."

"Never mind. You can have fancy birthday cakes when the rationing is over. Surely it can't last much longer."

One afternoon when I came home from school, Mother met me at the gate.

"Hurry up, Katie. We have to go to Miss Thomas' for your fitting."

I put my satchel behind the front garden hedge and we set out for Miss Thomas' home.

Miss Thomas greeted us with a mouth full of pins. She mumbled a greeting and ushered us into her workroom, where she deposited the pins in her pincushion. Helen's wedding dress was pinned together on the mannequin. My dress was hanging from a rack of other dresses.

Miss Thomas took it off the rack and held it up for me to see. "I found a scrap of plain yellow cotton in my scrap bag and I put a band around the waist and at the bottom of the skirt. Do you like that? It is only pinned at the moment so I can take it out if you want me to."

"Oh no, I like it. Thank you, Miss Thomas."

"Good. Take off your uniform and try it on."

I hurriedly took off my school blazer and dress and handed them to Mother.

Miss Thomas carefully put the dress over my head. "Be careful," she warned. "Don't get stuck on a pin."

She gently worked the dress down my body and turned me to look in a full-length mirror beside the window.

The dress came down to my ankles. Mother smiled at me. "Just what you wanted?"

"Yes, Mum. Just what I wanted, but I didn't know it would look so pretty." I turned and looked over my shoulder to see the back of the dress. The yellow band ended in a large bow at the waist.

Miss Thomas was busy adjusting seams and moving pins around. "There, I think that will be fine now. I am glad you like it. I'll sew it tomorrow and when Helen comes for her fitting, you can try it on one more time, just to make sure it is perfect. If it is, you can take it home. Now let me take it off. Put your arms up and just stand still."

She very carefully pulled the dress up and over my head. I was not pricked by one pin.

I put my dress and blazer on while Mother talked to Miss Thomas. "Thank you very much, Miss Thomas. You must put the cost of the extra material on the bill."

"No. No. It was just a scrap. I might never have found a use for it. Let it be my gift to Helen."

"That is very kind of you. I will tell Helen what you have done. Thank you again. Are you ready, Katie? Let's get home. We have to get supper ready."

Miss Thomas saw us to the door. "Goodbye, I'll see you and Helen soon, Katie."

"Yes. Goodbye, Miss Thomas. Thank you."

Helen came home on July the twenty-third, and the next morning, we went to see Miss Thomas.

"Come in, come in. It is good to see you again, Helen. How are the other wedding plans coming along?"

"Very well, I think. Mother has been very busy."

"I am sure she has. The wedding of her daughter must be exciting for her. I am afraid that I shall never be able to plan a wedding for a child of my own. I can only be happy for other people."

Helen's dress was not on the mannequin now. Miss Thomas went to a cupboard and brought out a cotton bag on a hanger. She lifted the bag off to reveal the dress. It glowed in the sun shining into the room.

"Here it is," said Miss Thomas. "It is still only sewed in running stitches, so that I can make sure it fits."

Helen took off her uniform and with Miss Thomas' help, put on the dress. The dressmaker stood back and surveyed her work. "How does it feel, Helen? It looks as though it fits you."

Helen twisted around in front of the mirror. "It feels great Miss Thomas. It fits like a glove. It's beautiful. Thank you so much."

"It is my pleasure, young lady. Now, shall we put Katie into her dress and see how you look together?"

Miss Thomas fetched my finished dress and helped me put it on. I joined Helen in front of the mirror and we admired ourselves.

"A prettier bride and bridesmaid I have never seen," said Miss Thomas. "Now let me help you take them off. Are you going to take your dress home, Katie?"

"Yes, please."

Helen's dress went back into its bag and mine was put in another bag for me to take home.

"Your dress will be ready to take home tomorrow afternoon, Helen."

"Thank you, Miss Thomas. My mother told me that you wouldn't let her pay for the extra material you put in Katie's dress. Thank you again. I hope you will be able to come to the church to see the wedding and your handiwork on display."

"Thank you, that will be very nice and it will make a little outing for Mother."

"Good. I'll see you tomorrow. Goodbye Miss Thomas."

I was already at the gate, but I turned and waved to Miss Thomas and called goodbye.

Miss Thomas waved back and closed the door.

"Helen, I feel sorry for Miss Thomas. She must be lonely."

"Yes, I'm afraid you are right. There are a lot of Miss Thomas's in Europe. The First World War killed so many young men that there were a lot of women who could not marry after the war. It seems an awful thing to say, but at least in the war that has just ended, as many women died as men did, so there will not be a large number of women left alone this time."

I did not know how to respond to that statement. It *was* an awful thing to say. How could any good come out of the war?

The last of the invitations were returned. Only a few of the invited guests could not attend. These enclosed money orders or cheques, in lieu of gifts, so that Helen and Joe could buy whatever they needed. Joe had three brothers. The eldest, Jim, was to be his best man and the two younger ones, Jack and Jeremy, were to be ushers. Father ordered a car from the car rental in town, to take mother and me to the church and then return to the house to pick up Helen and him. The week of the wedding the house buzzed all day, every day.

It was my last week of school before the summer recess and I was too excited to settle to anything. All I could think of was the wedding. Mother was a nervous wreck and went around the house asking questions that only she knew the answer to. Had she forgotten to ask anyone to the wedding who should have been invited? Was her cake good enough? Should she have bought a new hat? What would she do if it rained? Father took refuge behind his newspaper.

At last, the big day arrived. Mother was up at the crack of dawn and ran around trying to get father and me to do the same. She said Helen could sleep in, because she would have a tiring day. Having been wakened, I was too excited to go back to sleep and helped mother lay the table for breakfast. Father resisted, insisting that he didn't need to be ready at eight in the morning to escort his daughter to the church for her two o'clock-in-the-afternoon wedding.

Mother and I ate breakfast together and found ourselves sitting around afterward, wondering what to do. Father arose about eight o'clock and took a leisurely bath and shave before he ate. Mother insisted he call the car rental firm, to make sure they had the address and knew what time to come. I watched father make the call with his finger holding down the receiver button. He saw me watching and winked as he spoke to no one, in a voice loud enough for mother to hear in the kitchen. Helen had taken over the bathroom after father, and was now sitting in her housecoat with her hair beneath a towel turban. At ten o'clock, mother was convinced that she had given the wrong date to the florist and had to phone the shop immediately. The florist assured her that the bride's and bridesmaid's bouquets were already made up and her assistant was at that moment making the flowers for the buttonholes. The flowers would be delivered to the house by noon. The only thing left for mother to worry about was her cake.

She had carried it round to The Duck and Drake the day before, and she told us, given the publican strict instructions as to what he should do with it. "I bet he would have liked to tell you what to do with it," Father mumbled into his newspaper. Helen and I swapped grins.

At that moment, the front doorbell rang and mother rushed to open it. We heard her say, "Oh Jenny. Come in, dear. You've come to help Helen with her hair, haven't you? Helen is in the living room. Jenny's here, Helen," mother said ushering her into the room.

"Hi, Helen. How are you?"

"I'm fine. Mum is making me a bit nervous but I'll survive."

Jenny laughed. "I know all about that. My mother was as nervous as a dog in a cattery when I got married, and my wedding was Spartan compared with yours. Let's go to your bedroom and see what you want done with your hair."

They left and I felt abandoned. But not for long.

Mother caught my eye. "Go and take a bath and wash your hair. Don't get dressed. Jenny can do something with your hair, and then we'll have a quick snack and tea before we get into our wedding clothes."

When I had bathed and washed my hair, I went to Helen's room. I opened the door a crack and peeked round its edge. "May I come in?"

"Yes of course," Helen answered.

"Mum told me to ask Jenny to do something with my hair."

"Sure," said Jenny. "Sit on the bed while I finish Helen's."

Jenny put a couple of curls into place and turned Helen to face the dressing table mirror. "How's that, Helen?"

"Jenny, it's wonderful. You've missed your vocation. You should do hairdressing professionally. It would be ideal. You could work out of the house and save on babysitting fees. I'd recommend you to my friends."

"Do you think I could do that?"

"Yes, why not? You'd just do shampoos and sets at first. Then when you have a little money put by, you could take evening courses to learn cutting and all the other things hairdressers do. Your mum would be happy to babysit in the evenings, wouldn't she? Let's see what you can do with Katie. Come on Katie. You sit here and I'll go down and let Mum see my hairdo."

Jenny took the towel off my head and used it to dry my hair. She smiled at me in the mirror. "Now madam, how would you like your hair done? Do you want it plaited as you generally wear it, or curling around your shoulders; or would you like it piled on the top of your head? What are you wearing on your head?"

"A circlet of flowers. Why don't you do what you think would look good, because I don't know."

"All right. We can always start over if you don't like what I do."

She turned me round so that I could not see what she was doing. I could feel her making plaits on either side of my head and then the brush running through the rest of my hair. I shut my eyes and enjoyed the sensation. Jenny was so gentle, not like mother, who tackled my hair as if it were a barbed wire fence and moaned all the time about the tangles I managed to get into it. After a while Jenny said, "Where're the flowers you are going to have in your hair?"

"In my bedroom. On the bed with my dress."

Jenny ran off and came back with the circlet. She put it on my head and after a few more tweaks said, "There, let's see what you think of this," and turned me to see myself in the mirror.

Jenny held a hand mirror behind me, so that I could see the back of my head as well as the front. She had pulled the plaits up on either side of my head and wrapped them around inside the flowers like a crown. The rest of my hair hung down my back in soft waves and curls.

"Thank you Jenny. It's lovely. It makes me feel grown up. I wonder what Mum and Dad will think?"

"Let's go downstairs and ask them."

Jenny walked in front of me into the living room. "Ta Ra," she said and stepped aside to let me into the room.

Mum, Dad and Helen all looked at me in silence.

"Don't you like it?" I asked, disappointed.

"Like it. It's wonderful, but who are you? said Father. "Who is this beautiful young woman and what have you done with our little girl?"

I ran to Father and punched him playfully. "Oh Dad, you tease. Do you like the new me?"

"Yes, my love, I love you very much."

"Yes, you look wonderful, Katie. I shall have to be very careful or the people in the church will not notice me when you walk in," said Helen.

"You look very nice," said Mother. "But we must eat and then get dressed. You'll stay to have a bit of lunch, won't you Jenny?"

"Thanks but no. I'd better go home and help Mum with Joy or we won't get to the church."

Helen gave Jenny a hug. "Thanks so much, Jenny. When I get back for good, we'll sit down and discuss your future plans."

"I look forward to it. See you all later."

The flowers arrived as we finished eating and we all helped clear up the dishes and tidy the table. Mother took Helen and me upstairs to get dressed, while father put on what he called his glad rags.

Mother dealt with me first, carefully pulling the dress over my head. She even let me wear a dab of lipstick.

Then it was Helen's turn. She had put some powder on her face and lipstick on her lips. Mother draped a light piece of cloth over her head and face while she very gently lowered the wedding dress onto Helen's shoulders and arms. It fell to the floor in gentle folds of white satin. Next, mother slid the white pumps onto Helen's feet like the prince in *Cinderella* did and lastly, the veil was attached to the apple blossom headdress and placed on Helen's head. She pirouetted in front of the mirror.

"Will I do?" she asked.

Mother was shaking her head and crying.

Whatever is wrong now? I thought.

"Helen, you are gorgeous. Joe is a very lucky man. I am so happy for you but I hate the thought of losing you."

"You're not losing me. You're gaining a son. You would have liked to have a son, wouldn't you? Another man to tie to your apron strings?"

Mother laughed through her tears. "Now don't tease me, Helen. You know your father has never been tied to my apron strings, or he wouldn't have gone in the navy. And I was entirely happy to have two daughters. Boys are very boisterous. I appreciate a little bit of peace and quiet sometimes. Now you two go downstairs and I'll make myself presentable."

Father and Mother came down together. I thought they made a very handsome couple. Mother put a flower into father's lapel and he put one on mother's jacket. The rest, mother was taking to the church for the groom and his family. At the appointed time, the car arrived to take Mother and me to the church and then return to the house to collect Father and Helen.

Joe's family were already at the church. Mother put flowers in Jack and Jeremy's buttonholes, and gave them the remainder to give to Joe and Jim and their parents. Joe and Jim were sitting at the front of the church, but I had to wait in the entry for Helen to come. When the car arrived for the second time, mother gave me a last look-over, and went to take her seat across the aisle from Joe's family. Joe had kept looking round to see if Helen was coming. He looked a little nervous and I saw his face light up when mother took her seat and whispered something to him across the aisle.

Father took Helen's arm and I picked up the end of the veil. The organ began to play and we were off down the aisle.

I saw Miss Thomas and her mother, Vicky and Violet and their parents, some of my aunts and uncles and cousins, and several neighbours sitting on the bride's side of the church.

Joe and his brother stood as we came down the aisle, joining us when we reached them. Helen turned and gave me her bouquet to hold and Joe took her hand. The minister asked, "Who gives this woman to this man?"

To this father answered, "I do." He kissed Helen's cheek and went to sit beside mother.

I found this transaction a bit troubling. What gave father the right to give Helen to anyone? He did not own her. I determined then and there that I was not going to let him give me away. Then things got worse. The minister addressed the people in the church saying, "If anyone knows of any reason why these two people should not be joined in Holy wedlock, let him speak now or forever hold his peace." If someone did object, would the wedding be called off? I decided that if I got married I would definitely go to the Registry Office like Jenny did. It would also save mother a lot of grief.

After the ceremony ended, and Helen and Joe were declared to be 'man and wife,' I went with them, father, and the best man, to a room behind the altar where the adults signed a piece of paper to make it official. Then we came back into the church and everybody stood up and clapped as we marched back down the aisle, with the organ declaring that they were married.

Photos were taken, and at last we were driven to the Duck and Drake for the wedding breakfast. I was starving and glad when everyone was seated and the food was served. Telegrams were read and toasts made. I enjoyed clinking glasses with everyone I could reach. I was even allowed to have a drop of wine and water, to do it with. The larger cake that Mother had made was cut by Helen and Joe, brandishing a large knife, and then it was taken away to the kitchen. Mother told me that the smaller top cake would be kept for the christening of Helen and Joe's first child and the larger bottom cake would be cut into small pieces by the publican's wife, to be distributed in small cardboard boxes to each guest. She also whispered in my ear, "If you put the cake under your pillow when you go to bed tonight, you will dream about the man you will marry."

Jack and Jeremy produced a gramophone and a stack of records, put on a record, and the strains of a waltz drifted across the room. Joe and Helen took to the dance floor. After they had circled the room a couple of times, Jim came over to me and said, "May I have this dance?" I froze. I had only danced in the church hall with spotty little boys, and here was a handsome man asking me to dance.

Mother pushed me from behind. "Go along Katie."

Jim took my hand and led me onto the floor. One hand around my waist and the other holding my hand, he expertly guided me around the room. Helen and Joe waved at us as we passed them. I was floating on air. Soon, Joe's parents and mother and father were dancing, and in a few minutes, the guests had joined us. Jim steered me faultlessly through the crowd, never once stepping on my toes. I was on Cloud Nine and wished the music would never stop. When it did, Jim took me to one of the chairs that had been spread around the room. "Thank you for the dance, Katie. I enjoyed dancing with you, but now I must borrow your sister for a dance."

"Thank you," I said. "That was the best dance I have ever had."

"I'm glad. I know it won't be the last," he replied.

Another record was on the gramophone; father was dancing with Helen, and mother with Joe. I watched enviously, my toes tapping to the rhythm. The music stopped and another record began to play. This time it was a polka. Mother and father came and sat beside me and I saw Joe heading toward us.

"Hey, Katie. Come and polka with me," he called. "Your dad can have the next waltz. More suitable for a man of his years," he added with a grin. I looked at father. He pretended to be fierce but I could see that he really was not offended.

Joe and I flew around so fast that I was often off my feet and was red in the face when the music stopped. Dancing with Joe was nothing like dancing with Jim. Jim was romance; Joe, wild abandon. When Joe returned me to my chair, father laughed. "I have to admit you were right Joe. Tell your brothers to put on a slow dance next."

I danced a waltz with father and Jim had been right. I was not a wallflower. There were several cousins from my family and Joe's, who danced with me, and I had to rethink about the kind of wedding I would like. Could one have a dance after a Registry Office wedding?

At seven o'clock, Helen and Joe went to a room upstairs, to change into street clothes before leaving for the honeymoon. When they came back, all the unmarried women stood together in front of Helen. Helen turned her back on them and threw her bouquet over her head. Many hands reached up to catch it. In the scrabble, it was impossible to see whose hands had managed to hold it. The women who had failed to catch the bouquet drifted away, and Jenny stood alone, clutching the flowers to her chest. Helen looked around and clapped her hands when she saw her. She ran to her and hugged her. They both cried and laughed and Joy came running to be picked up. Helen hugged them both and ran back to Joe.

The families kissed Helen and Joe goodbye and we all went out to see them into the taxi that father had called. I was sad to see them go, but I had had a wonderful time that I would always remember. I felt much more mature than I had when I got up that morning. It was just as well that I took what mother had said about the cake with a large pinch of salt, because when my head hit the pillow, I only dreamed of dancing all night. I couldn't possibly marry that many men in one lifetime.

Chapter 21

Helen and Joe came home on August the fifth. So many houses had been destroyed during the war, that it was almost impossible for newly-weds to find any place to live. Helen and Joe would live with us. Father and mother had removed Helen's old bed from her room and replaced it with a new double bed.

The next morning, Joe dressed in his uniform and returned to camp. I was delighted to have Helen to myself again. I am afraid that in my happiness, the fact that people were still fighting and dying in the Far East did not even register in my consciousness. It came as a great shock to me when the news reported that at 8:18 a.m. on August, the sixth, an American B-29 bomber, the Enola Gay, had released an atomic bomb called Little Boy, over the Japanese city of Hiroshima. The news of the destruction and death it created was horrifying, making the Blitz seem like a minor mishap. When on August ninth, news of a second bomb, Fat Man, being dropped on Nagasaki reached us, we could not believe it had happened. The two cities had been turned into Hell on Earth. My faith in a loving God took another dip.

On August fifteenth, the Emperor of Japan announced that Japan had surrendered. The formal surrender ceremony took place on the deck of the USS Missouri, on September 2nd, 1945 and the Second World War finally came to an end.

If I thought that this was the end of the horror, I was sadly mistaken. As the Allied soldiers advanced across Japan, they encountered the prisoner of war camps and internment camps where captured soldiers and civilians were treated more like animals than humans. Once again, we saw pictures of dead, dying, and barely alive skeletal men, women, and children; victims of a society that believed surrender was shameful and death was the only viable option.

Helen's comforting words about the future were not entirely convincing. Only time was able to put the past behind me and let me think that better days would be ahead. Joe was demobbed in October, and he and Helen set up home with us. They helped Father repair the damage done to the inside of the house and get the garden back to its pre-war state, with a flower garden and a smaller vegetable plot.

Gradually, life returned to normal, and I decided that it was time to remind Mother of the promise she'd made that I might have a dog and maybe a rabbit, when the war ended. This involved a family conference, since now there were two families living in the same house, and on Saturday morning, we gathered around the kitchen table.

We still had the chickens in the garden, which provided us with more eggs than we needed. Rationing was still in effect but father suggested that we keep only enough hens to supply our own needs and thus lessen the workload.

"You, Katie have enough homework to keep you busy and with fewer hens, we can get rid of two henhouses and have a place for Joe to grow his own vegetables. It should be well fertilized."

Joe grinned. "Yes it should. Thanks, Dad. I'll feel better if I can contribute to the food supply."

"Is that okay with you, Katie?"

"Yes, if I can have a dog. And we keep Clucky."

"We'll take a vote. All in favour of us getting a dog say, Aye."

Five 'ayes' rang out, loud and clear.

"Passed," said Father. "Does anyone have any thoughts about what kind of dog we should have and where we should buy it?"

"Yes, I have," said Helen. "I think we should go to the RSPCA and pick one that looks as though it needs a good home. I don't care what breed it is."

"That sounds good," said Father. "What about you, Katie? Did you want a puppy?"

"I had thought of a puppy, but I don't really mind. Perhaps we will find a puppy that needs a good home. Do you know, Dad, whether Bob would accept a puppy better than an older dog?"

"I don't know, Katie. We can ask the people at the RSPCA. They will probably be able to help us with that. Anyone else have thoughts on this?"

There were murmured 'no's' around the table.

"Right, when will we do this?"

"Today!" I shouted. I decided to leave the rabbit for another time.

That afternoon we set out to buy a dog.

The lady at the RSPCA welcomed us with open arms. Sales had not been brisk and she had still been getting animals that families no longer wanted. Most of the cages contained kittens, which brought forth 'ohs' and 'ahs' from Helen and me.

Mother firmly tore us away from them saying, "We're here to get a dog, remember?"

There were only three cages with dogs in them. None of the dogs were puppies, so whether to take a puppy or an older dog was no longer relevant.

The first cage housed a small, white, fluffy terrier with bangs hanging over its eyes; the second cage was filled by a large, very thin dog curled up head to tail, looking at us with large sad eyes. The lady said it was a greyhound. In the last cage was a long-haired dog smaller than the greyhound and larger than the small one. It came to the front of the cage cocking its head and wagging its tail. Father asked the lady how old each dog was and which dog would be likely to accept living with a young cat.

"The greyhound is the oldest. She was a racing dog and is too old to race now. The little terrier and the collie are younger, two or three years old. They are both popular family dogs, but the collie generally gets along well with other animals. This one is a bitch and was sharing a home with her mother. The owners found they couldn't feed two dogs and felt the younger one would find a new home more easily than the mother."

"Thank you. I think that will help." Father turned to the rest of us. "Well does anyone have a preference?"

"I don't want the little one," said Mother. "I find very small dogs like that one yap a lot."

"I feel very sorry for the greyhound but she's a bit big and after all that racing, I suspect that the poor thing will either need walking very fast or not want to walk at all," said Helen.

"She may not live much longer either," Joe added.

"What about you, Katie?"

I would have taken them all. The little terrier was cute and I worried about what might happen to the greyhound if nobody wanted her. The collie was a lovely dog and she had just been taken from her mother.

"I don't know. I want them all."

I saw mother about to speak but Father got in first for once. "Sorry Katie. We can only have one dog. So far we have one vote to not take the terrier and two votes to not take the greyhound. Can I have someone vote to take one of the dogs?"

"Which one do you like, Dad? After all, this is to replace Ollie who was your dog," said Helen.

Father looked as though someone had pricked his balloon. He obviously did not want to be responsible for making the choice any more than the rest of us. "Thank you, Helen. You are always the voice of reason."

He paused and walked slowly past each cage. The greyhound was sleeping and the terrier scratching itself. The collie tried to lick his fingers through the cage mesh. "Since nobody has rejected the collie," father announced, "and since she is the only one that has come to inspect us, I propose we take her home. All agreed?"

"Agreed," we said in unison.

The lady came to remove the collie from her cage and father attached Ollie's old lead to the collar around the dog's neck. He read the name on the dog tag and said, "Hello Daisy. Welcome to the Wells and Birch families."

We all patted her and got our fingers licked in thanks. "Come along. Let's go home," said father. He strode to the door with Daisy walking at his heel, tail wagging furiously.

I was still worried about the greyhound. On the way out, I stopped to ask the lady what she thought would happen to her.

"Don't you worry, dear. If nobody takes her I will. I can't bear to see an animal put down. She'll die peacefully in my home."

"Thank you," I whispered and ran to take Daisy's lead from father.

PART TWO

———— ❖ ————

I never did get a rabbit. Daisy and Bob got along very well and soon Helen announced that she and Joe were going to have a baby. They still couldn't find anywhere to live and when a baby boy arrived, I felt that if I had one more piece of joy in my heart, it would burst. The baby was called John and was surrounded by so much love he never had to cry for more than a second.

The war had ended but it was a long time before much changed. In 1946, bread, the one staple that had not been rationed during the war, was rationed. On the first day of rationing, I was the only customer in the baker's shop who had remembered to take the bread coupon.

It was 1948 before the end of rationing began. Bread and flour were the first to go. 1949 saw the end of clothes rationing followed in 1950 by canned and dried fruit, chocolate biscuits, treacle, syrup, jellies, mincemeat, and soap. Tea, the one thing (other than Winston Churchill) that had stiffened the English backbone throughout the war, stayed rationed until October 1952. Children had to endure candy rationing until 1953, when sugar rationing also ended. It was 1954 before we could throw away our ration books.

While Germany received monetary aid from America, Britain struggled to recoup its losses. For years, the only goods in the shops were 'seconds,' with the good china, furniture, and clothing being designated 'export only.' Men returning from the forces to their pre-war jobs were determined to make better lives for themselves.

The unions became stronger and strikes broke out in one industry after another. I remember thinking that the unions were going to do what Hitler had failed to do; crush our spirit. Electricity would be cut off without warning. Coal was short one winter because there was no one to deliver it. I remember pushing my doll's pram to line up at the railway station to fill it with coal that was piled there, awaiting delivery. We used the coal dust in the coal shed mixed with cement and water to make brickettes, which glowed red as they got hot and then crumbled into grey ashes. One night, when there was no more coal dust, Father and Joe took turns sawing up bits of wood from Father's shed. They sweated profusely while Mother, Helen, and I shivered in the living room.

In 1947, the whole country was cheered by the announcement that Princess Elizabeth was to be married to Prince Philip of Greece and Denmark. During the war, the Royal Family had endeared themselves to the people of London by refusing to move out of the city and visiting those whose homes had been bombed. The palace and/or grounds were hit sixteen times between September 1940 and March 1941, and in June 1944, a V-1 flying bomb struck the grounds, palace walls and an eighteenth-century summer house. Princess Elizabeth had joined the army and learned to maintain and repair military vehicles and ambulances and Prince Philip had fought in the Mediterranean and Pacific during the war, having joined the Royal Navy at eighteen in 1939. By the time he married Elizabeth, he had reached the rank of commander. His royal background, handsome figure, and his naval career seemed ideal for Elizabeth and their union a true love match.

Clothing was still rationed and women sent their clothing coupons to the palace to help with the purchase of a wedding dress. These were returned with handwritten thanks from the princess because the government had allowed her 200 extra coupons for her dress. Philip renounced his royal title of Prince of Greece and Denmark and became a naturalised British subject, adopting the surname of his British uncle, Lord Mountbatten.

The wedding of Princess Elizabeth and Lieutenant Philip Mountbatten took place on November twentieth, in typical November weather; dull and damp. Joe and Helen volunteered to take me up to the Mall to watch the wedding procession. There was no television allowed in the Abbey but the BBC was going to record the proceedings and mother and father opted to stay at home in front of the fire and babysit John. Helen, Joe, and I set out on the evening of November nineteenth, with blankets, food, and thermos flasks of hot tea. There were hundreds of people making the same trip and it took us a while to find a spot on the kerb from which we could see the flag flying from the top of the palace.

The night was damp and we were glad of our blankets as we huddled together for warmth. Sleep did not come easily. There were people coming and going all night, chatting and laughing, sometimes bursting into song. Policemen mingled with the crowds and kept the peace. I managed to fall asleep at some point and when I woke, the morning had arrived. There were even more people sitting and standing the length of the Mall. Helen handed me a cup of tea from the thermos flask and two biscuits. The sky was still grey. I had no idea how long we had to wait before the wedding procession started, but time did not seem important. I had never seen so many people gathered together. It was exciting and a little frightening.

At some point, the police stopped walking around and lined up at kerbside, two-arms' length between them. A murmur of excitement ran through the crowd and everyone stood up. At last, we heard cheering coming from the direction of the palace. The cheers grew louder and we could see small flags waving in the crowd ahead of us. Joe stood behind me between two policemen so that I could see a stretch of road. I poked out my head and saw a carriage coming toward us. "They're coming," I called above the cheers. Two horses passed and then the carriage was in front of me. I saw the queen waving through the window and then she was gone. More carriages passed with more waving people. The noise of cheering became louder, accompanied by the flapping sound of the small flags that people were waving.

Two carriages with the bridesmaids and two small boys passed and we heard the cheers increase in volume. I thought it could not get louder but it did. The crowd began to move as those at the back tried to get a better view. The police linked hands and leaned back into the crowd, and Joe gripped my shoulders to keep me upright. The coach rolled in front of me and I saw the princess and the king sitting inside. Princess Elizabeth looked beautiful, with a shining tiara on her head and a big smile on her face. Then they were gone.

A few people in the crowd began to collect up their belongings and leave, many of them walking toward the palace. I turned to Joe and Helen. "What do we do now?"

"That depends on what you want to do," said Helen. "We can go home or we can stay here and see the procession come back to the palace. I expect some people will then go to the palace to see the princess and Philip come out on the balcony."

I tried to remember how long Helen and Joe's wedding ceremony was but could not. I was feeling tired and cold, but I would have liked to see Princess Elizabeth with Philip. I looked at Helen and Joe. They looked as exhausted and cold as I was. "Perhaps we should go home," I said. "Unless *you* want to stay."

Joe and Helen looked at one another and laughed. "I think we should stay to see them return to the palace and then leave," said Helen. "We would only see very small people on the balcony. Let's stand up for a bit and stretch our legs."

And that is what we did. I saw Philip and thought he was very handsome.

Unhappily, in 1952, the king died. He had lived to see the births of Charles and Ann, ensuring that the monarchy would continue for yet another generation. The people of London grieved as hard as they had cheered the wedding five years before. Nineteen fifty-three saw Elizabeth crowned and once more, the streets were filled with cheering crowds looking forward to a new Elizabethan era.

Gradually my life settled into a comfortable rhythm. The years passed and nobody dropped another atomic bomb on anyone. The

Americans continued to make and test the bombs, which many years later proved to have caused illness in some of the soldiers exposed to the fallout. The Russians began to build atomic bombs too. Churchill proclaimed that a 'Cold War' existed between that country and the West.

Helen and Joe managed to buy a small house in one of the 'new towns,' which had been created by the government to replace some of the ones devastated during the war. Mother was devastated to see them go. "I won't see little Johnny if you move," she moaned.

"Of course you will," said Helen. "You can come and visit us. We're not going to the end of the universe. There's a very efficient railway service almost to our door." After the move, Father and I suffered through a week or two of deep sighing and the occasional weepy episode, but a phone call announcing that another grandchild was on the way soon had Mother smiling again.

Seven months later, the phone rang early one morning and Father, always an early riser, answered it. I could hear him saying, "Hello Joe... that's good...everything is okay?...Yes she hasn't come down yet...yes I will. Oh here she is I'll put her on."

"Who is it?" asked Mother.

"It's Joe. The baby's arrived."

"That's wonderful. Is it a boy or a girl?"

"I don't know," Father admitted.

"Oh, give me the phone for goodness sake. What have you been talking about?" She grabbed the phone from Father's hand and almost shouted into it. "Joe, great news. Is the baby a girl or a boy? A girl, how lovely. How much did she weigh?"

In a matter of minutes, Mother found out the time of birth, how much the baby weighed, how much hair she had, what colour it was, that the baby did not have a name yet, and that Helen and the baby were both sleeping. Best of all, she was given an invitation to visit to help with the baby and John. When she put down the phone, she went immediately into organizing mode.

Father sighed. "Right Katie. We're on our own now. Your mother will be busy packing and shopping and getting into a spin so my advice to you is to find something you absolutely must do somewhere else."

Father was right. Three days later, burdened with suitcases of clothes and various packages of baby gifts and home baking, we were on the train to visit Helen, Joe, Johnny, and the new baby. Mother was in her element; offering advice that mostly went out with the baby's bath water; rocking her when she cried, although no-one else had heard the crying; suggesting names; and encouraging John to make friends with his baby sister. After two days, father and I went home, leaving mother to stay behind and help until Helen and Joe could manage without her. She phoned father every night to keep him up to date on the baby's progress and bemoaned the fact that the "poor child still doesn't have a name." I think that Helen and Joe may have decided Mother would not go home until the baby had a name, so they decided to call her Jennifer. Mother was back with us two days later.

I began to feel safe from an imminent third world war breaking out, but a war of a different sort was raging in my conscience. Why had my family been spared in the war and Jenny and Joy deprived of a husband and father? We were no better than them. How could I trust a God who would let this happen? My belief in a loving God was not strengthened by events happening around the world. I still went to the church services on Sundays with father and mother, but questioned what good it did. It seemed that the human race was incapable of living together in harmony.

Thousands had died in India when the country was partitioned because of religious factions. The Irish Catholics and Protestants were killing one another in Northern Ireland and the I.R.A. members were blowing up the English in England. The partition of Korea after the war eventually led to the Korean War in 1950, and a decade later, soldiers acting as peacemakers were the only thing stopping the Greeks and the Turks killing one another in Cyprus. So many innocent people had died in war in the first twelve years of my life. I kept asking myself; why, if God is all-powerful why does he, or she, let this happen?

After Grammar School, I trained to be a nurse and took a further course to become a qualified domiciliary midwife. There was an enormous rise in the number of births, as the men who had been fighting the war came home and married, started families, or added to the ones they had before the war. The hospitals were soon overflowing and restrictions were put on who could give birth in them. Only first-time mothers and those who had experienced problems in a previous birth were admitted. I soon had a thriving practice, which could demand my presence any of the twenty-four hours in a day.

The shortage of houses, or any accommodation after the war, made it practical for me to live with my parents. It was also a joy to have someone cooking my meals or providing a cup of tea when I came home after a particularly long delivery. I loved seeing the joy of the parents when the new baby was put in their arms. It was rare for a full-term baby born at home to die, and I only experienced one in twenty-two years. On that occasion, I once more questioned why God allowed such things to happen.

My work did not provide much leisure time, and the men I met on the job were always already spoken for. I did not marry but my work satisfied my maternal instincts, and I developed a loving connection with my nephew and niece. I sometimes worried about what their future would hold and despite my ambivalent feelings about God, prayed to him or her that they would not have to live through another world war.

My father died in 1970 and five years later, my mother developed cancer and quietly slipped away from me. I realised that I was now free of obligations to anyone. Helen and Joe were happily living their lives together, and John and Jennifer were adults, not needing a loving but sometimes annoying aunt telling them what they should and should not do.

Jenny had made a new life for herself. She took up Helen's idea of becoming a hairdresser. She put ads in the small, local, shop windows, advertising cutting and styling, with a recommendation from Helen alongside a picture of her at her wedding. Helen, Mother and Aunt Em told everyone they knew about the venture and soon, Jenny had a steady stream of customers. She did so well that in a few years she had enough money to be able to open a little salon. She also remarried when Joy was seven years old, and added two more children to her family. I had kept in touch with her, but she would not miss me if I was not around.

I had a school friend whose family had emigrated to Alberta after the war. When I suggested to her that I would like to visit, she agreed enthusiastically. I fell in love with the open spaces and wide blue skies and upon returning to England, set about applying for jobs in Alberta. I found that I would not be able to work as a nurse until I took a nursing degree at the university. I would be almost fifty by the time I finished the degree, but the retirement age was sixty-five not sixty, as in Britain, which would give me seventeen years to earn a little pension. My parents had left the family home to me and it would bring a good price. I could afford the fees to take a nursing degree and if funds got low, I would get a part-time job somewhere.

I applied for a place in the nursing faculty and was accepted. The house and furniture were sold and a year later I arrived in Edmonton, as a landed immigrant. I started my courses in September and my only regret was that there were no home births in Edmonton.

I was surprised by the number of churches of various denominations in Edmonton. I remember standing at a four-way crossing, one day, with a church on every corner. Canadians were more religious than the English it seemed. I used to go to church with my parents when they were alive but after mother died, I stopped going. I had watched the congregation getting smaller and smaller until I was the youngest person there. The female vicar had two churches to look after, presumably because the offerings were not enough to pay for two people.

I loved Edmonton; the river valley and its parks, the beautiful summers, and even the winters with all that sun and clean, white snow so dry it could be brushed off one's coat like talcum powder. I learned to ski on a man-made ski hill in the centre of downtown, and hiked along trails through woods that made me feel that I was in the countryside. I also loved the Edmontonians. Unlike the reticent English, they welcomed me with open arms. My courses at the university were easy, since I had already learned what they taught. Even the young students accepted me as one of them, and I soon had a crowd of friends. Once I had received my degree, I applied for jobs in all the hospitals. I was accepted in the Royal Alexandra Hospital, where to my delight, doctors requested my presence in the delivery rooms, once they found out I had been a domiciliary midwife in Britain.

My school friend became like a sister and we now spend many hours remembering and laughing about our childhoods. Helen and Joe have visited several times, and I am hoping that someday, John and Jennifer will bring their partners and my great-nieces to see me.

Many years have passed since I watched that ceremony on the beaches of France and many more, since I started to put my life on paper. Ever since World War II ended, there has been a war of one kind or another being fought somewhere in the world every day; nation against nation, tribe against tribe, religious sect against religious sect. Canadians went to Afghanistan as peacemakers, but they have killed and been killed for more years than the Canadian forces fought in the Second World War. The First World War was called the 'war to end all wars.' I fear the present one may be 'the war that could not end.'

I am still fighting my personal religious war. In the church we attended in England, there was a picture of Jesus surrounded by children. Underneath was written, "Suffer the little children to come unto me." As a child, I was puzzled by the word "suffer." I know now that it also means 'allow,' but when I consider the use and abuse of young children as soldiers in the recent wars in Africa, I feel the more generally accepted meaning of suffer is the correct form in that inscription.

The Jesuit maxim, "Give me a child for his first seven years and I will give you the man," is a dire warning to us all.

As I write this, it seems that we are involved in a fight for the survival of humankind. If there is a God who created our world, it seems that he or she has tired of us and is doing everything possible to drive us to extinction.

This is not without precedent. Remember Noah?

Barbara Azore

I was born in 1934 in the County of Middlesex which is now a borough of London, England. The war had started when I began my elementary schooling in September, 1939 and it ended in the year I finished elementary schooling in 1945. I carried a gas mask in a cardboard box to school everyday for the first years of the war and we practiced sitting in the classroom in the masks. There were air raid shelters in the school field and during the Blitz when the planes dropped bombs day and night we sometimes had to have our lessons in them. I do not remember much about life before the war but the war I remember clearly.

I came to Edmonton, Alberta in 1967 and have lived here ever since. I had two sons and a daughter and it is their children who started me writing. I wrote stories for them to accompany picture sweaters that I knit for them.

Barbara Azore is my real name. My grandfather baptised me and gave me the name Azore. All I know of its origin is that my grandfather "plucked it from the Heavens." I have never met anyone else with that name so when I had some articles published in the Edmonton Journal Newspaper I decided to use Azore as my 'nom de plume'.

I have published three children's books under the same name. In October 2006, McNally Robinson, New York, made *Wanda and the Frogs* their Book of the Month.

Printed in Canada